The Ideal Countess

KATHERINE GRANT

This is a work of fiction. Names, characters, places, and incidents either are the product of the author's imagination or are used fictitiously. Any resemblance to actual persons, living or dead, events, or locales is entirely coincidental.

First paperback edition January 2020

Interior book design by Asya Blue
Book cover by Julia Gerbach

ISBN 978-1-7343813-0-6 (paperback)
ISBN 978-1-7343813-1-3 (ebook)

www.katherinegrantromance.com

Chapter One

Miss Alice Winpole's first ball was almost everything she had dreamed it would be.

There was the footman at the door, bellowing ancient family names so she could peer over at the viscounts and barons and even one duke as they entered. There was the string quartet in the corner that never played a note out of tune, unlike the overeager fiddlers her mother hired for their country parties; the instrumentalists featured an olive-toned violinist who Alice was sure had been imported straight from Milan. There were ladies swathed in precious silks and gentlemen in their richest suits. Couples young and old slipped through double doors for fresh air on the Romanesque patio. Alice's mother had even whispered that there were orange-flavored ices in the refreshment room.

For a first ball, it was surpassing all of Alice's expectations, which were quite considerable since she'd been hearing about the splendor of the Season for the entirety of her seventeen years. The ball was perfect, in every way except one.

Alice had not yet been asked to dance.

Her parents, the Baron and Baroness of Eastley, had coached her on this. For the exact same amount of time that Alice had been hearing about balls, she had also been happily ensconced in their country seat of Bleneccle Manor. While her father undertook the five-day journey to London a few times a year, it was far too long—and far too likely that a coach wheel would break and the ladies would be stranded in a one-room inn—for him to invite the family along. Her mother had warned Alice that since they were so remote in their corner of the north, it would take a few weeks to properly introduce Alice so that gentlemen *could* ask her to dance. Alice had been fully prepared to stand against the wall during her first ball for one or two dances.

But things were not going according to plan. Alice and her mother were supposed to have arrived a full week before this first ball of the Season, thrown by the Marchioness of Leighstor, so that her mother could take Alice around on morning calls to meet the matrons of society. But first a wretched rainstorm had delayed the start of their journey by two days, and then on the highway through Nottinghamshire a carriage wheel *did* break. The carriage-maker in town was laid up with what Lady Eastley called an unmentionable disease, so they had to wait another two days for the fix. By the time Alice set eyes on London – loud, messy London – there had been barely enough time to present her to the queen much less anybody else.

And so, Lady Eastley and Lord Eastley had deposited Alice against the very wall where she still stood before melting into the crowd to find her some dance partners. Playing the part of Marriage Mama, Lady Eastley chatted with fellow matrons, angling for introductions to their sons or nephews or brothers in hopes she could then introduce said gentlemen to Alice. Lord Eastley, meanwhile, had decamped to the cluster of males in the card room, promising to send every eligible male her way.

Alice had more faith in her father. While Lady Eastley was pretty and polite, she didn't have many connections, and she far preferred chatting over tea to rubbing elbows with London's *ton*. In the ballroom, she was being relegated to the quietest of conversation circles. In contrast, Lord Eastley knew more people in London, and he was the type of friendly boisterous that made people want to like him. Many times at home, Alice had observed a tenant or laborer come to Papa with a complaint, only for the man to leave laughing with a compromise as a solution.

Yet despite her parents' efforts, the caller had already announced the first minuet, a quadrille, and a polka, and Alice remained with no introductions. She glanced at her dance card as fellow debutantes walked arm-in-arm with gentlemen to begin the polka. At the start of the evening, she'd written her name at the top in her brightest lettering, excited to see the card fill up. Now there were only eight more dances until supper, and every line was still blank. Indeed, the card itself was beginning to shrivel from all her fidgeting. Soon there wouldn't be a way for gentlemen to claim a dance, even if they wanted to.

Alice peeked at her fellow wallflowers. There were five or six others lined against the wall. At first, Alice had tried to make conversation with them – in truth, tried to make friends with them – but apparently the fate of the wallflower insisted on no conversation. The other ladies were almost all older than her, one of them surely over twenty, and wore dim colors or long faces. The one farthest from Alice had even pulled out some knitting. Surely in her new peach-pink gown, Alice stood apart. She kept her body angled toward the dance floor, a hopeful yet demure expression on her face. Certainly, any observer must see that she didn't belong with the wallflowers. Soon she would have an introduction, which would lead to another, and before she knew it, she would be the talk of the town.

If she'd been back at Bleneccle Manor, this wouldn't be a problem. Even if no one asked her to dance, Alice would simply march up to an available gentleman and ask him herself. But in London, everything was different. She was here as a member of peerage, to find a husband of good standing, and so she would act every part a lady.

The polka came to an end. Alice tried to look happy for the dancers as they laughed and clapped and turned to their next partners. There was absolutely no way under any circumstance that she would acknowledge the knot in her stomach, the one that got bigger and sorer every second she remained unnoticed. She was the daughter of

Lord Reginald Winpole, Baron of Eastley, and she had no feelings except pleasant ones. In fact, even if the whole ball passed and she spoke to no other soul, she was determined to enjoy it.

Alice was so set on enjoying the ball that she didn't even notice a man approaching until he was right beside her.

"Miss Winpole, what a delight to see you here this Season."

Lord Hugh Osborne, Earl of Windemere, their neighbor to the south by twenty miles, bowed before her.

Somehow, instead of jumping out of her skin in surprise, Alice managed a responding curtsy, as if she spoke to gentlemen at balls all the time. Of course, she *had* spoken to Lord Windemere at balls before, since he was always invited to Lady Eastley's Christmas balls. She had spoken to his lordship at meals, too, and on horse rides and even one time shared a coach with him and his mother.

A few years older than she, Lord Windemere was the type of boy who barely saw past his own glasses. He was always reading a book or sketching inventions on spare paper. The last time she had seen him – a few years ago, before he went off to Cambridge – all he could talk about was his belief that England could prevent a revolution if only they invented new farm tools. Terrible Alice, in fact, had wished him well at university and whispered as he'd walked away, "Don't come back!"

Yet now, Lord Windemere was the best thing she had ever seen. His hair was longer, the color of chestnut and curling as a frame to highlight a sculpted face: sloping cheekbones, slender nose, and eyes that were a piercing blue even through his thick round spectacles. He seemed to have grown a few inches, too, and his shoulders were thicker, stronger. In her haze of gratitude, Alice found him so handsome that her breath caught at the base of her throat.

He was commenting something about the ball, and she completely missed it. She smiled to make up for it. Lord Windemere's eyes darted to the blank card in her hand. "Do you by any chance have this quadrille available?"

Alice blushed. "Yes, thank you."

He took her hand to lead her to a place in the dance line. His grip was firm yet gentle through the kid skin gloves they both wore. Alice wondered if she would notice how every gentleman led her to the floor, or if she was only so aware because this was her first dance in London. When they reached their respective places across from one other in the two lines, Hugh winked at her, and Alice blushed again.

The quadrille was not Alice's favorite dance. At home, she preferred the galop because it required such energy to leap from one foot to the next. The quadrille was too stately, less of a dance than a choreographed walk. But as the violin played its first chords and the caller announced the first steps, she began to appreciate the careful tempo. At Bleneccle Manor, Alice had no need for conversation. Here at the marchioness's ball, the quadrille gave her every excuse to speak not only to Hugh but also to the other dancers. Between Hugh's polite questions about their journey and how long they planned to be in London, she was passed to an earl, a baron, and a viscount. She overheard *their* conversations with their partners. The earl even asked who her father was, which nearly promised an introduction later. It wasn't a dance at all, and yet she finished just as breathless as if she'd done a jig.

Lord Windemere claimed her hand again. He led her not to the wallflowers but to her mother, who was in a throng near the front, chatting with their hostess, Lady Leighstor. "Oh Lord Windemere, how clever of you," Lady Eastley exclaimed. "I didn't know you were here, otherwise I would have said good evening much sooner."

"It was a surprise to myself as well," Lord Windemere said. "Made even more pleasant when I discovered that my favorite neighbors are in attendance. I hope you don't mind, but I did impose on Miss Winpole for a quadrille."

Lady Eastley beamed, first at him, then at Alice. "That's so kind of you. I know she has quite been looking forward to dancing."

Alice's smile tightened. *Why* did her mother have to make her sound so pathetic? Lord Windemere had already found her in the bouquet of wallflowers. There was no need to hammer home the point that no one else had asked her.

Lord Windemere surprised her by turning back in her direction. "In that case, perhaps I can have the upcoming galop as well? If I recall, it is your favorite of the London dances."

Blinking, Alice tried very hard not to be speechless. Her mind raced to understand how Lord Windemere could possibly know what her favorite dance was, much less make the distinction between the fashionable dances and her true favorite, the regional jigs that would never be allowed in a London ballroom. If she opened her mouth, she would sputter, rather than give the gracious "I'd be delighted" that she *wanted* to say.

Before she could align her brain with her mouth, Alice was surprised again, this time by her father clapping a hand on Lord Windemere's shoulder. "Pleasure to see you, Windemere, but I'm afraid Miss Winpole's galop is spoken for."

Lord Windemere stepped back, making way for Lord Eastley to join the group. And *he* made room for yet another addition, a man Alice had noticed the moment he'd been announced to the ball. Tall, muscled under his silk coat, dark of hair and eyes and expression.

The Duke of Cornwall.

Even Alice, who knew nothing about the *ton*, had heard of the duke. He'd just returned from the West Indies, where it was whispered he saved ten men in a battle to subdue local rebels. That he was an eligible duke had gotten everyone at the ball in a dither.

And now Alice's own father had secured an introduction.

"May I present my daughter, Miss Alice Winpole, Your Grace?"

The duke bowed over her hand, lifting his gaze to hers only as his lips met her glove. She felt the kiss as if it were a sear into her skin.

"At your service, my lady. When I saw you dancing so divinely with Osborne here, I knew I had to claim a figure for myself."

His words thrilled against her skin as surely as if he had touched her. Alice curtsied, smiled, tried not to show how flattered she was. Vaguely, she heard the musicians strike the opening chords.

"I believe that music is ours," the duke said. Even his voice was low, a bass thrill through Alice's body. She followed him to the dance floor. His grip was much stronger than Lord Windemere's, a vise around her hand that said he never wanted to let go. Alice quite lost her head: the Duke of Cornwall himself held her hand. Looked her in the eyes. Made her heart thump dangerously.

As the dance started – as her deepest fantasies of a ball in London came true – it was only in the back of Alice's mind that she registered Lord Windemere exiting the room, hat and greatcoat in hand.

Chapter Two

Hugh was quite relieved to take leave of the ball early. He had never been one to enjoy an overcrowded London residence, no matter how many dances or card games there were to entice him. His mother had failed to train him on how to delight in small talk, nor had she convinced him that all these dozens of acquaintances he saw a handful of times were excited to see him. He subscribed to the logic that since he wasn't interested in the lords and ladies of London, they certainly weren't interested in him.

No, he was quite happy to have used Miss Alice Winpole's distraction in the arms of the Duke of Cornwall as a reason to retreat. Although he did wish she'd been whisked away by some other man – really, any man besides the dreadful duke.

He chose not to think too hard about the ball as he waited for his driver, nor while the carriage tottered ten minutes through Mayfair to return him to the stately Windemere townhouse. Nor did he plan to revisit his reservations about the Duke and Miss Winpole as he changed from the silk suit into his rougher corded trousers. Yet even as he descended the stairs to his basement workshop, Hugh discovered the couple was still on his mind. Namely, the wide-eyed expression of delight on Alice's face as the Duke whirled her onto the dance floor.

She certainly hadn't looked at *him* that way during their quadrille.

Hugh shook his head. These were the types of thoughts he did not indulge and were precisely the reason he stayed away from any type of sociable event beyond public lectures. Overall, he was lucky Alice had set her eyes on the duke instead of him: now he could make a tidy report to his mother and return to his better workshop in Cambridge, or perhaps even his best workshop at home at Richmond Hall.

Although, if Cornwall was anything like he'd been at school – and the years thereafter, for that matter – Hugh worried perhaps Alice shouldn't set her cap on the duke.

I saw you dancing with Osborne...

But no, Hugh couldn't believe the celebrated duke would still harbor a grudge over the stuff of schoolboys.

Better to mind his own business and tinker on with his inventions.

He'd just tied his leather apron across his chest when behind him a prim throat cleared. Hugh nearly jumped out of his skin.

"Mother, what are you doing here?"

From her perch in the back corner of his workshop, Lady Windemere glared at him. "I live here, do I not?"

She wore her nightclothes, ensconced in the opulent velvet robe he'd given her the past Christmas to keep warm. In the dim candlelight – which he'd assumed his staff had lit in anticipation of *his* needs – she had been sewing, no doubt another needlepoint pillowcase to remind him to *Honor Thy Parents* or *God Save the King*.

"I thought you would already be asleep," Hugh said, choosing not to point out his discomfort that she should trespass on his private workspace.

"I am not." Lady Windemere let him wither in the bald statement for a moment before continuing. "The more pertinent question is what are you doing here? Are you not supposed to be at a ball?"

At least he could satisfy her there. Tired of the subject already, Hugh set about his work: opening his notebook, collecting his instruments, lighting more candles to improve his sight. "I went to the ball, as you requested. I danced a quadrille with Miss Winpole and asked for a second dance, but her father intervened and introduced her to the Duke of Cornwall. As you can imagine, the prospect of a rich, handsome duke was much more exciting to her than another dance with me. I fear she is quite lost to him."

"After one dance?" His mother angled the words so he would feel their stupidity to his core. "I can't imagine what Lord Eastley is thinking, exposing his daughter to such a rake. Everyone knows His Grace would remove to India rather than marry, God bless his poor mother's soul."

"Perhaps Lord Eastley thinks Alice is winning enough to change His Grace's mind." After all, she had been one of the beauties of the ball. Hugh couldn't believe his eyes when he'd finally found her huddled with the wallflowers, already four dances into the evening. The little Alice he'd known as a neighbor was gone, replaced with a stunning young woman: golden hair that gleamed in the candlelight, slender figure accentuated in a perfect pink dress, and eyes that sparkled with something beyond the usual excitement.

Why no one yet had danced with her, he couldn't say, but for a moment there as he walked with her around the room, he saw his mother's plan as brilliant. How could he *not* want to marry the glittering woman Alice had become?

But that had been only for a moment. Throughout the quadrille, Alice's eyes had roamed, soaking up everything around them except for him. And she could have said yes to the galop before her father intervened, if only she hadn't hesitated. Didn't that moment – that endless second when she simply blinked at him – spell it out? Hadn't he understood even then that she was only glad to have had a dance? That the excitement on her face had never been for him, or about him, or remotely near to him?

Hugh's mother was speaking, and he should have been paying attention. "It is her first ball of the Season, Hugh. No one meets their husband at their first ball, or if they do, they don't realize it until the end of the Season. You should have stayed through supper, at least. Even when Alice dances with someone else, you can still woo her parents. Lady Eastley has always liked us, but I dare say Lord Eastley is setting his sights as high as possible for Alice. You'll want to be there to talk him down to earl."

Hugh had never before felt that earldom was too low a rung in the world. How he hated this marriage game. How he hated all of society.

"We'll call on them tomorrow," Lady Windemere said, "and set things back on track. I think I can manage that, at least." She paused, as if expecting an answer. He wondered if she hoped he would cheer. "That is, if you still want to put a smile on your old mother's face?"

She did know how to turn a phrase. Hugh took her hand and kissed it goodnight. "Your hopes and dreams are safe with me."

"You have always been my favorite son." Lady Windemere rose, the barest of smiles on her lips. It was the old joke between them, since he was her only son, though she had borne eight children.

More to the point, he was the only child who had lived past the age of six.

Small favor it was to make her happy, when he could see all her losses etched into the lines of her face and stoop of her shoulders. She patted his hand, then retreated up the stairs. At the door, she turned. "Have you eaten anything?"

"Of course," he lied.

"I'll send a tray down. Don't stay up all night again. You don't want Lord Eastley thinking the circles under your eyes are from staying out at vice dens."

"No," Hugh agreed. "Only the Duke of Cornwall could get away with that."

She may have found it funny; Hugh was already deep in his notebook again and did not wait for her reaction. But a few minutes later, as he soldered a piston to an axle, he heard the echo of his own words and thought of Alice, lost in the eyes of a rake. If only…

But he did not indulge in such thoughts.

Chapter Three

There was no better cure for a sleepy debutante than tea with her mother and sister. Though Alice had felt positively dreadful when she first awoke at midday, the sunny front room of their parlor, the familiar bone china of their tea service, and the deliciously delicate cakes served by Cook were doing wonders to perk her up. So too was her family's excitement to relive every perfect detail from the night before.

"I'm quite jealous that I never had a Season," her sister Margot, Countess of Wickham, declared after hearing how the Duke of Cornwall had stolen Alice away from Lord Windemere. "Previously I counted myself lucky not to have gone through it, but now it sounds less like an ordeal and more like a fairy tale."

Five years older than Alice, Margot had been preparing for her Season when their distant cousin, the soon-to-be Earl of Wickham, came to stay for the month of March. It had taken precisely one match of whist for Geoffrey to fall madly in love with Margot, and they were married by April. But that was just the way things went for Margot. She'd inherited Lady Eastley's dark hair and sculpted cheekbones, so that when Alice stood next to her sister, she felt like a doll brought to a party of real girls. Margot walked the line between feminine charm and masculine humor that led to charming a man into marriage during cards, rather than offending him, as Alice would likely have done.

"Good thing you'll be at the next ball," Lady Eastley said, adding another pour of brisk Assam tea into each of their cups. "We mustn't rest on our laurels. The dance with Cornwall was a compliment, absolutely, but he's known for his capriciousness. Margot, you must help us secure more introductions so Alice can make the best connections."

Alice helped herself to a warm currant scone. She was doing her best to ignore the little twinge of apprehension that plagued her every time her parents mentioned the need for marriage. Growing up, she and Margot had done nothing but dream of what it meant to be a London debutante: the gowns, the food, the dancing. Certainly, there had been dashing gentlemen in their fantasies, but marriage was beside the point. Of course, the stories they told ended with a proposal, or with happily ever after. The finality of an actual marriage – a man she would be handed to, entrusted to, forever and ever – had always seemed as far away as London itself.

But here she was. In her Season. In London. The gowns had come true. The balls had come true. Last night, she had danced with the most dashing gentleman in London. Come August, if not sooner, Alice would likely be married.

It was enough to make her slather the scone with

Cook's rich clotted cream. She reminded herself that she could do no better than to have her own two parents as her guides. Their marriage was the product of a Season, and they were the picture of happiness. They wanted nothing more than to find her a husband who would give her the life they felt she deserved.

Marriage, she reminded herself, was the key to a lady's happiness.

Margot and Lady Eastley were discussing the upcoming social calendar: there were three balls to choose from the next night, picnics, concerts, a play, not to mention the social calls they needed to make. Alice tried to focus again on how exciting it was, since in the country she would be doing nothing other than planning which novel to read next.

Stuggins, their butler, interrupted with a short bow. "The Dowager Countess of Windemere and the Earl of Windemere wish to pay a call, my lady."

Alice's stomach fluttered. She had not expected anyone to call on them after their first true day in London. That it was Hugh and Lady Windemere made it feel more than ever like a playact: here they all were, pretending to be a part of the Season.

"Of course, show them in. And send in more tea, if you please." Lady Eastley shooed Margot over on the settee so that she could sit next to her, leaving the better seats for their guests. Lady Windemere walked in first, chin held ever so high, though her shoulders caved in more than Alice remembered. Behind her trailed Lord Windemere, looking more like his usual apprehensive self. Alice couldn't help noticing again how well his hair set off his face. It was almost as if to remind the viewer that yes, he was actually handsome despite the spectacles, thank you very much.

She rose with her mother and sister and bobbed them a curtsy in greeting. Lady Windemere nodded, then promptly sat down in the seat Alice's mother had just vacated. "So, Miss Winpole, you have come out."

Alice always remembered too late why she dreaded visits from the Osbornes: Lady Windemere's strange way of expecting answers to statements. She dropped her eyes to her tea, fumbling over the best response. "Yes, ma'am."

"We attended her first ball yesterday," Lady Eastley chimed in. "Of course, we saw Lord Windemere there. What a wonderful time, wasn't it? Alice danced with seven gentlemen. I daresay she was among the most popular of the young ladies."

That was an exaggeration. Alice still remembered that painful first hour against the wall. She glanced at Lord Windemere, to see if he showed any visible objection to her mother's characterization. He only looked down at his plate, which boasted half a scone and two of Cook's almond cakes.

"I can see why. You have a good figure, a pleasing face. Competent manners." Lady Windemere's gaze zipped Alice's spine even straighter. "Not to mention a decent family name and dowry."

Surely her words were a compliment, yet Alice couldn't quite bring herself to say thank you. This was the sort of conversation that had earned Lady Windemere a reputation across Cumbria as the Cold Countess. They said she couldn't keep a housekeeper for more than a year, so severe was she with her criticism. Alice had even heard that for one housekeeper, whose youth and beauty Lady Windemere had coveted, the countess had paid a visiting gentleman to put her in a ruinous position, so that Lady Windemere could dismiss her without pay.

In this moment, Alice opted for the safety of silence. Margot filled in for her, "I quite agree, Lady Windemere. It should make for an eventful Season. What do you wager, three marriage proposals by June?"

From everything Alice knew of Lady Windemere's severe demeanor and exacting expectations, she expected Margot to earn herself a cutting scold with the remark. Instead, Lady Windemere chuckled. "A guinea says it will be four."

Alice looked to Lord Windemere for his reaction to this spark of humor, which tilted towards inappropriate. He'd been watching his mother, but as Alice glanced over, his gaze turned to hers. She jerked her face down, a blush rising almost immediately to her cheeks. His blue eyes were too piercing, even shielded by the glass spectacles. Just in that one instant, she had the strangest sensation he could see past her excitement, straight into the jangle of nerves twisted deep inside her.

"I quite agree. The only thing lacking is introductions," Lady Eastley was saying.

"That should clear itself up with time. The real concern is…" But Lady Windemere didn't finish her sentence. Her words caught on a cough, which turned into hacking, which turned into wheezing. Lord Windemere was on his knees beside her in an instant.

"Mother, are you all right?" His voice was soft as it always was, though Alice had never before noticed its depth, how it ran to its bassline with the steadiness of a river. "Perhaps some brandy?"

This question was directed to Lady Eastley. Alice hopped up, as she was closest to the red lacquer cabinet where Lord Eastley kept a decorative glass bottle of Madeira. "Will this do?" She poured it into a snifter without waiting for an answer, then rushed it to the Osbornes. Lord Windemere accepted it, his fingers brushing against Alice's for the merest of seconds. And just like the night before, Alice's heart leapt, and she wondered if this was what always happened when a man's skin contacted hers.

"Thank you," he said.

Lady Windemere sipped the drink, and slowly her fit waned. When she could breathe again, she lifted her chin back to its usual height. "I do apologize. You can see why I myself did not attend the ball last night. My health is not what it used to be."

"I'm so sorry to hear of it," Lady Eastley said. "It was

kind of you to visit this afternoon. We would have come to you, only I didn't realize you had accompanied Lord Hugh to town."

The countess waved her hand in the air, uninterested in the niceties Alice's mother had to say. "The real concern you should have for Alice is making the right connections. I heard she danced with the Duke of Cornwall last night."

Alice's heart thudded faster. It had, indeed, been quite the dance. She remembered the duke's hand at her waist, pulling her ever closer, the dark look in his eyes and charming smile on his lips, the way he made her feel he clung to every word she said. And, mingled into that heady memory, was the fact that Lord Windemere had disappeared nearly as soon as she'd accepted the galop.

His lordship now busied himself with returning his mother's Madeira snifter to the cabinet, twisting shut the bottle that Alice, in her rush, had left open. Alice held her breath, afraid of what would come next from Lady Windemere's mouth. A rebuke for ignoring her son? A congratulations for snagging London's most eligible bachelor? Advice for how to entice him into marriage?

"I could scarcely believe it myself when I heard it," Margot said. "Another guinea that the Duke himself offers marriage?"

This time, Lady Windemere did not chuckle. She set her stern gaze on Lady Eastley. "You do not spend time in London, so I'm sure you do not know his reputation. His

Grace is a rake, through and through. He has no business looking at Miss Winpole, so much as dancing with her. You'd be wise to keep them apart, lest he tempt her into ruination."

Alice couldn't quite keep her jaw from dropping. For one thing, the Duke of Cornwall had been nothing but respectful for the entirety of their dance. He was seven steps away from the throne, after all; he had more breeding than Lady Windemere in all her severity could ever hope for. For another, Alice was not a simpering idiot who could be led into some scheme by any kind of rake. The very idea that Lady Windemere felt it necessary to leave her sickbed to warn Alice's mother – after hearing of one dance – ignited such rage that Alice resorted to biting the meat of her tongue to keep from saying things she would regret.

She settled, instead, for glaring at Lord Windemere. It was plain he was the one who'd told his mother of the dance. He must have inflamed the tale with such color that his mother felt driven to action. Never mind why he should choose to do so – Alice hadn't the faintest idea. She only knew it was completely mortifying and utterly unforgiveable.

In this one fell swoop, she made her resolution. She would never speak to Lord Hugh Osborne, Earl of Windemere, again.

Chapter Four

Though he wasn't looking at her – he'd been doing his best throughout this whole charade not to look anywhere – Hugh could feel Miss Winpole's anger emanating straight at him from her seat beside the tea table. He didn't blame her. He knew how his mother's words sounded: overdramatic and ill-informed. He also knew that logic concluded he was the original source of the gossip flaming her fire. Still, he wanted to hold his hands up as a shield, to plead innocent to Alice's condemnations. He wanted to explain.

But there was no explaining Lady Windemere. He knew that from twenty long years as her son. Lady Eastley obviously knew it too – no doubt from twenty-five longer years as his mother's neighbor – for rather than argue, the baroness of Eastley simply nodded along. "You are too kind to look out for us, Lady Windemere. I confess, I hadn't realized how out of touch I am with society until last night, when I entered the ballroom and recognized next to nobody. I only know the Duke of Cornwall for his infamous victories in the West Indies."

Hugh heard what was said between the lines: *leave off, I'm not interested in gossip.* He yearned to leap to his feet and announce the interview over. He'd never had patience for social calls, and this one was too fraught for comfort. When he'd agreed to accompany his mother, he'd expected some motherly matchmaking, not an offensive attack on Miss Winpole's reputation. But just as he was not the man for dancing or socializing, nor was he the type of man to rudely insist his mother leave just because he'd had his fill.

Luckily, Lady Windemere seemed to be reading the same message as him. Flatlining her lips into a smile, she rose – shakily – to her feet. "Soon you'll have so many offers, you won't remember this dance with Cornwall anyway."

"Indeed," Lady Wickham said, trying once again to use her trademark joviality to defend her sister from his mother. "And I'll be sabotaging the fourth gentleman who dares offer for Alice so as to win our wager."

Hugh's mother took his arm. "In the meantime, Hugh will keep an eye on Miss Winpole. Won't you, dear?"

He couldn't help it – his eyes went straight to Alice. She looked at him, too. In a way, she was as lovely as she'd been the night before in the duke's arms: her cheeks blushed red, her green eyes wide and bright. Only then, she had been staring up at a man in joy. What Hugh was receiving was pure hatred.

He looked away. There was nothing to do but nod along with his mother. Smile at Lady Eastley. Bow to Miss Winpole on his way out. And ignore that deep, whirling wish that somehow or another he could reverse her emotions.

His mother's plan had never been malicious. It was hardly even a plan, so much as a suggestion. She'd summoned him to her chambers in January, just before he returned to Cambridge, and laid out the grim news: she had fluid in her lungs, the doctor didn't know how long she would last, and she'd like to see him married before she died. "I know you've been distracted by your plan for revolution and all that, but isn't there *some* lady who has caught your affection?"

It was a cruel time to ask him such a question. Hugh was so distraught over her diagnosis that he said the first name that came to mind: Alice. Of course, it wasn't simply a name that popped onto his tongue. He'd admired Alice since he'd first started noticing girls, when at the Christmas ball she listened to his plans for inventing a machine to clear the roads of snow rather than get trapped in country houses for days on end, and her response was to ask if he could also invent a candy better than peppermint sticks.

But his mother had reacted as if he harbored a deep-seated love for the girl, when really, he thought about her from time to time, mostly when on the road home in the snow or whenever he smelled peppermint. Yes, she was beautiful; yes, she was smart; yes, she was funny; yet that didn't add up to Hugh pining to marry her from the bottom of his heart.

Still, when the Season came around, Lady Winde-mere had written: *Make your mother happy and have a*

June wedding, won't you? She'd arranged to open up the house, ordered his new wardrobe, even accepted invitations on his behalf. And when he'd complained about the Marchioness of Leighster's ball, she'd said, "Just dance with Miss Winpole, won't you? That will be enough to make me happy."

He should have known that wasn't true. Lady Windemere had never been known to be happy unless she had her way.

Chapter Five

Hugh spent the next four days blissfully ignoring his mother's project in favor of his own. While he'd never quite figured out the snow machine he'd bragged about to Alice, he had developed quite the career of inventions over the past five years. At Eton, his focus had mostly been on small improvements for himself: an automated fan run by a pulley weight system, a hot box to keep foot stones warm for his bed in the winter, even a parachute for escaping out his third-story bedroom window (used mainly to sneak back into the library for further studying).

Then at Cambridge, he attended public lectures on history and the plight of modern England in addition to his full-time studies in engineering. While his fingers couldn't keep from sketching new ideas, his mind was captivated with a bigger picture. What stood between English nobility and the guillotine? Why couldn't men, in this wondrous age of steamboats and lightning rods and electric capacitators, find a way to make crops more reliable so that the common people could rest easy knowing they would have food in their bellies? For that matter, why not use modern invention to improve on putting roofs over heads and money in pockets?

The problem at Cambridge had been that Hugh was

too busy studying what other men had already accomplished to apply effort to his own ideas. It was only now as a graduate that his inventions could take the form of revolution, as his mother was so fond of saying.

His focus for the spring was a machine to make it easier to harvest hay. Just as one used scissors to cut hair in swaths rather than one follicle at a time, Hugh supposed there was a more efficient way to collect hay than to send twenty tenants into the field with scythes.

And so, in the aftermath of Miss Winpole's anger, Hugh ignored his mother's suggestions to go to this salon or that ball, and instead hunkered into his basement workshop. It was drearier than the ones he set up in Cambridge and Richmond Hall, but it was still, for him, a paradise. Against the one wall, a drafting table with wide sheets of paper awaited his sketches and notes and calculations. Opposite stood his tool chest, a gleaming pine armoire with glass doors to display his wrenches, screwdrivers, irons, saws, hammers, and more. Proud in the center of the room was his worktable, as thick as a butcher's block, thoroughly scratched from his various endeavors.

Hugh needed only to open the door to feel more relaxed; with each step down the staircase, more stress shed from his shoulders. Here, he did not need to puzzle out how to make his mother happy, nor did he need to parse his feelings about losing the last and most precious member of his family. The problems of the world – poverty, starvation, riots – consumed him in a much more manageable way than the twistings of his lone human heart.

It was in the middle of such a day, just when he was affixing his full set of pistons to the rest of his engine, that his butler interrupted with a calling card. "Are you home to the Duke of Cornwall, my lord?"

Hugh blinked at the card in confusion for a number of reasons. One, he'd been under the impression it was still the early hours of the morning, though now he noticed a luncheon tray on his drafting table looking thoroughly ignored. Two, he'd never received visitors before; they always came for his mother, and his presence was optional. Three, he and the Duke of Cornwall, as a rule, didn't speak.

"Certainly," he responded to Alby, who promptly collected the luncheon tray as well as Hugh's answer. "I will receive him once I've washed up a bit."

But the duke's voice rolled down the staircase. "No need, Osborne. I'm fascinated to see your little cave."

His steps clacked loudly on each stair from the fashionable leather boots that shone on each foot.

Hugh clapped on what he hoped was a polite expression. "Would you care for some tea?"

Cornwall's face was by now visible, so Hugh could see the grimace. "Don't you have anything stronger for a war hero?"

It was not for lack of introduction that Hugh didn't speak to Lord Alan Dupree, the famed Duke of Cornwall.

Indeed, the problem was rather the opposite. They'd first met when Hugh started at Eton: as head boy, Alan considered it his duty to break in the new students by all means necessary, and his favorite victim had always been Hugh, since the latter was prone to reacting with tears and snot streaming down his face. For revenge, Hugh had laced invisible cords through Alan's trousers for the final assembly of the year, so at the very moment that Alan rose to lead the school in a chorus of *God Save the King,* Hugh tugged at his secret line and Alan was suddenly quite exposed, drawers and all, to the entire school.

From Hugh's perspective, the feud could have ended that moment. But Cornwall was eighth in line for the throne, the first and only son in his household, and a revered bully. Rather than laugh it off, he set his cronies on Hugh to make his years at Eton more miserable. He wrote Lady Windemere with fabricated stories of Hugh's vices. He even mentioned Hugh by name to the Prince Regent as a "waste of gentleman's blood."

Hugh had hoped that Cornwall's two years serving the crown in the West Indies had washed him of any remaining hostility, but he dared not presume. For the moment, he opened the lowest drawer in his tool chest and withdrew a bottle of Scotch whiskey. "Will this do?"

Cornwall took the bottle and swigged without waiting for a glass. In Hugh's estimation, he drank quite a bit more than was appropriate for a social visit in the middle of the afternoon.

"So, you still tinker with your toys, eh?" The duke picked up a wrench and poked at Hugh's motor. Only the muscle memory of worse abuse kept Hugh from flinching.

"I heard you saved ten men in the battle for the West Indies," Hugh said, opting for a more mature conversation than they'd ever had. "Congratulations."

"Some will say I saved a hundred." Alan put the wrench down and moved to peer at the drafting table. "All in the service of the crown. Say, why haven't you joined the Navy yet?"

There were a hundred answers Hugh could give, ranging from the truth – he didn't need to – to the sentimental – his mother would never allow it – to something a veteran might want to hear – he'd only muck up the battlefield rather than help. But Hugh couldn't quite judge what Alan wanted to hear. They were no longer children; their taunts should be years behind them.

Instead, Hugh kept his silence. He examined Cornwall, the war hero, the most eligible bachelor in London. He supposed he could see the appeal: Cornwall was tall and strong, with fierce expression and dark eyes. If he peeled back the years, Hugh could almost remember the excitement he'd felt when he first met the head boy, who would one day be a duke. He'd thought Alan tracked his every word, that he was actually fascinated by Hugh's description of how the canal locks worked, that perhaps Alan was the answer to the older brother Hugh had always longed for.

"I suppose you prefer to clutch to your mother's skirts," Cornwall sneered. "How would you live if you couldn't visit her every fortnight?"

It occurred to Hugh that Cornwall might never have taken the opportunity to grow up. Leading men in combat didn't necessarily mean he had fought all the battles of his soul yet. Hugh decided to try a new tactic. "You know, my lord, I suppose it is high time I apologize for that nasty prank. It was horrid of me. The only excuse I have is that we were schoolboys."

Snapping to attention from the draft table, Alan summoned a sneer only generations of breeding could produce. "I haven't the slightest idea what you mean."

Hugh bowed his head. Deference, he'd found, was almost always the best answer.

"Perhaps it's not your mother's skirts you are so fond of," the duke said, lifting a hammer from the worktable. "Perhaps you have finally graced London with your presence to find other skirts behind which you can hide. Miss Winpole is quite becoming, is she not?"

Hugh's fingers curled to a fist instinctually. He'd suspected the duke's comment on meeting Alice – *I saw you dancing with Osborne* – was some sort of insult to him, but he hadn't wanted to believe it. He'd hoped his view on the whole encounter was as dated as scratched spectacles, cracked with his personal history with the duke. Now a fiery heat stoked his belly; Cornwall could torture Hugh all he wanted, but the duke had better have enough sense to leave an innocent lady alone.

"Did you come here merely to discuss the marriage mart?" Hugh did his best to match the duke's sneer.

Cornwall poked at the pistons again. "I've been gone a long time. I thought I'd make sure you hadn't forgotten about me."

The words, which would sound so sincere and polite from anyone else, dropped like lead bullets into Hugh's stomach. But before he could respond – as if he could find an appropriate response – the door at the top of the stairs opened again, this time bringing an interruption from Lady Windemere.

"Your Grace, I do apologize. Nobody told me you were visiting, or I would have rescued you from Hugh's dark workshop much earlier. Have you had your tea yet?"

Cornwall snapped back into the role of duke in an instant. The ugliness of his sneer smoothed into a dandy's smile. The menace of his shoulders retreated to a gentleman's practiced nonchalance. He bowed to Hugh's mother.

"The apologies are mine, Lady Windemere, for I cannot stay."

They devolved into chatter as Cornwall bounded up the stairs. Hugh watched him go, listening to his voice get smaller and smaller as he retreated through the house. If only the man himself could disappear like that.

Hugh turned back to his pistons and sighed. It was time to put his project aside, again. He had a Season to attend.

Chapter Six

When one decided not to listen to one's nosy neighbors, Alice discovered, the Season could be quite enjoyable. She went to balls three straight evenings in a row before begging off the fourth, too exhausted to contemplate pinching her feet into dancing slippers again. In the mornings, Margot visited with her two little ones – George and Valentina with matching blond ringlets – and pored over the fashion magazines or gossiped about the latest scandals with Alice and Lady Eastley. In the afternoons, Alice and her mother flitted from one salon to another, exchanging tea with countesses and marchionesses in neat, quarter-hour intervals. When the sun peeked through the clouds, Lord Eastley took all three of his ladies for rides through Hyde Park. Everywhere they went, Society was all too happy to welcome Alice into its folds as the next Successful Marriage.

Indeed, Alice couldn't quite believe her dream Season was playing out so easily. She was a practical girl and had expected more hiccups. She was *supposed* to have a harder time of it, like spending more time as a wallflower, so that she could savor the good things all the more. Yet aside from that first ball, and Lady Windemere's rude warning, Alice's Season was unfolding according to plan.

She'd even made a friend amongst the throng of

young ladies elbowing each other out of the way in the marriage mart. The daughter of a marquess, Miss Lisbeth Dawes always wore a foot-high feather in her hair to make up for her lack of height and kept a wicked comment in her back pocket to send Alice into spirals of giggles. In fact, it was with Miss Lisbeth Dawes that Alice surveyed the crowd at the afternoon *musicale* hosted by the Viscountess of Fairfax.

"There's the Earl of Thorne," Lisbeth commented, a slender nod in her subject's direction to illuminate her sentence. "Didn't he dance with each of us twice on Thursday?"

"My father is quite certain an offer will be coming soon." Alice suppressed a giggle. The earl had actually danced with Alice three times at the Cavendish ball, and he'd sent a bouquet of pink carnations the following morning. But he was old – his grown son was also making the rounds for a wife that Season – and known to be deep in gambling debts, to boot.

"Why, so is mine. Did you get the same carnations?" Lisbeth kept her voice light and innocent as her lips spread into a wicked smile. "The poor earl does so want to add a dowry to his coffers."

"I only hope he doesn't get hauled to the poorhouse over sending us flowers." It was a terrible thing to say, yet Alice couldn't help herself. It sent them both into an unladylike fit of laughter. Lisbeth clamped her hand on Alice's forearm as they drew glares from the matrons, including

Lady Eastley.

"Now in the other corner, we have the Marquess of Asbury." Lisbeth almost accomplished the same nonchalance she had mastered earlier, except for a few wheezes between her words from catching her breath again. "I noticed he took you for a breath of air in the garden at the Portland ball. Do tell: did he steal a kiss amongst the garden hedges?"

Alice squared her shoulders as if she *had* been kissed and needed to hide it. "To be honest, I was quite shocked. He had the audacity to spend the whole time..." She paused for dramatic effect. Lisbeth leaned in, so Alice even lowered her voice to a whisper. "...describing his four-year-old's toothache to me."

Lisbeth had to pretend a sneeze to cover the guffaw that shot out of her. Lady Eastley stalked over from her conversation with the Marchioness of Leighster. "Young ladies, I do believe you are here to stimulate the gentlemen, not each other. Miss Alice, perhaps you have noticed that the Earl of Windemere is here. I expect you'll make yourself available to greet him."

This time, Alice's spine straightened in anger. Lord Windemere had conveniently made himself scarce since his mother's accusation, so Alice had only needed to contemplate her anger when tossing around in bed. Now here he was, following up on Lady Windemere's promise to "watch over" Alice. As if he were some great chaperone. As if Alice's own mother wouldn't guide her properly.

She spotted him now, finishing his polite words with their hostess and moving towards the back wall. Lord Windemere did not walk comfortably through a crowd: his shoulders caved forward, his neck downward, and he paused incessantly to make way for everyone else. Alice wanted to scream at him to stand up straight. Except, of course, she didn't want to say anything to him at all.

She caught a flash of his eyes – still intensely blue, even from far away – and looked away. If not for her mother's recent warning, she would have *turned* away. She had no interest in an earl who spread malicious rumors to his mother, neighbor or not.

Their hostess, the Viscountess of Fairfax, rang a silver bell to entreat everyone to find a seat. Alice followed her mother through the throng; they hadn't quite planned strategically, and instead of getting the coveted front seats where they could be admired by all through the whole concert, they ended up in a middle row.

"Sit straight and don't ever look bored," Lady Eastley reminded Alice. Then she threw a smile across the room at Lord Windemere, who sat at the edge of the third row. He nodded tightly and didn't look at Alice.

The musicians started their first piece, a new composition from the Austrian Mozart. Alice tried to focus on the music: the neat order of it, the sweet violin, how the notes floated through the room like sunlight. But then Lord Windemere fidgeted, and her anger shot back.

What Alice hadn't figured out – even after night

upon night of not sleeping over it – was why Lord Windemere was so bothered by her one dance with the duke. At first, she'd thought perhaps Lord Windemere harbored intentions for her: he'd been the first to ask her to dance, and he'd wanted the galop as well. She remembered vividly his smile when he first found her. He'd taken her hand so gently. In her memory, Lord Windemere had beamed through the quadrille, even though he didn't love to dance.

But this theory had been quashed when Lord Windemere had fallen off the face of the earth after that one tea. Alice had been quite happy to write it off, since she didn't know what she would do if faced by a suit from the earl. He was handsome enough, once one looked past his spectacles, with those strong cheekbones and a thoughtful brow and eyes that burned so intensely blue. More than handsome enough, she was willing to admit when lost in the privacy of her thoughts. And he *had* made her jitter when he'd taken her hand, which, now that she was a veteran of more than a week into the Season, Alice knew did not happen every time a gentleman led a lady through a dance.

Still, Alice couldn't quite forgive that he would spread such nasty gossip to Lady Windemere that she would feel the need to question Alice's morals. If Lord Windemere *had* been interested – which Alice now concluded he wasn't – Alice certainly didn't like the idea of being married off to a man who put stock in chattering about people behind their backs.

Applause returned Alice to the Fairfax salon. She joined in the polite clapping that signaled the end of the first movement.

As the pianoforte carried them into a calmer, more regretful second movement, Alice supposed it was time to turn the question to herself: why did Lady Windemere's accusation make her so angry? Alice's own parents should be the ones claiming it familiar to a fault. Lady Windemere was implying they were inept at shepherding Alice through the Season, which was quite a charge. Yet Lady Eastley and Margot had laughed over it once the Osbornes left, and when Lord Eastley heard the story, he only smiled fondly and shook his head. "Pay her no mind," he'd advised. "If the Duke of Cornwall compliments us with his affections, we are happy to take them."

Lest he tempt her into ruination.

Those were the words that seared through Alice's head at any quiet moment. But now, with the violin commandeering the mood, she had to admit that perhaps it wasn't purely anger she felt. There was a thrill that accompanied her reaction to Lady Windemere's words. A thrill that Alice could only parse as a mixture of fear — and excitement.

For wasn't that what she'd felt, dancing that one galop with the duke? His hands holding her tight, his face so perfectly handsome, his gaze dark and secretive and locked on hers. The whole time, her heart beat too fast, and Alice couldn't tell whether it was from the dance or the duke. He'd said so little, asked her no questions, but his attention was on her for all of those five minutes. And at the end, he had apologized, "I wish I were a better conversation partner, but your beauty has left me speechless."

Even remembering the dance dampened Alice's hands with excitement. Lady Windemere was right. The Duke of Cornwall *did* tempt Alice.

Applause again, and now they were on to the third and last movement. This one was cheerful and fast, a whirlwind just like the Season. Alice couldn't believe it had not even been a fortnight yet. All it had taken was the dance with the duke to get her introductions; the Marchioness of Leighster whispered to Lady Eastley at a dinner the night before that Alice was one of the prizes of the year. Alice, the marchioness predicted, would have her pick of husbands.

And who did Alice want? She closed her eyes, cleared her mind, then posed the question to herself. She almost gasped, so scared she was of the result. One Duke of Cornwall, handsome and brooding and looking only at her, for the rest of her life.

When she opened her eyes again, she caught Lord Windemere gazing at her. He turned away too quickly, his attention locking onto the musicians. Alice smiled. Given this new insight, she supposed she could be more forgiving to Osborne. Whatever his reasons for stirring

Lady Windemere into a froth, he'd been picking up on a kernel of truth: Alice did harbor wicked marriage intentions towards the duke. She couldn't hold it against him, nor did she need waste energy on anger. Lord Windemere could do what he would. Alice was going to pick her own husband. If he came over to "keep an eye on her," Alice would treat him as the old family friend that he was. Let Lord Windemere worry about whatever feelings he had for her.

Chapter Seven

Hugh had forgotten the agony of sitting in a salon chair for a whole hour. One did not fidget when sitting in a salon, nor did one get up and stretch one's legs, or lean forward to ease one's back, or even sneeze. A lady could wave her fan in slow, modest rotations; a gentleman did not have that excuse. The only movement that would not telegraph offense toward the hostess was discreet head turns to admire fellow attendees, though these should be strategic so the other attendees taking looks themselves didn't notice whom one was looking at.

To return to the word he'd thought of at the beginning of the concert: *agony.*

When finally the concert came to an end, Hugh shot to his feet, not because he felt so strongly that the musicians merited an ovation but because he needed to return the flow of blood to his lower half. So happy was he that the music was over that he almost forgot his true mission. Somehow, he needed to deliver Miss Alice Winpole another warning about the duke.

She was even more stunning that afternoon than the other two times he'd seen her so far. At the ball, standing with the wallflowers, she'd been pretty but contained, coiffed appropriately yet somehow still looking the country bumpkin. At tea, she'd been quite comfortable, though perhaps overtired. But now – after a week of, by all reports, taking the *ton* by storm – Miss Winpole was radiant. Her whole being sparkled with enthusiasm. Even if he hadn't been planning on speaking to her, Hugh would have been drawn to her like a magnet to its pole.

Which meant, of course, he had to wait his turn. She and Lady Eastley patiently handled her throng of callers: the Earl of Thorne, complimenting her dressmaker; the Marquess of Asbury, requesting a turn in the park soon; Misters Frampton and Umber and Padsworth; and of course the omnipresent Marchioness of Leighster hovered not far away. The latter, waiting with Hugh, leaned her silver head towards him in a conspiratorial whisper. "Miss Winpole is quite the conquest this Season, is she not?"

Hugh tilted his head. The marchioness was the revered gossip of the *ton*; reveal anything to her, and she would magnify and worsen it and tell it to the whole world in the same conspiratorial whisper. He settled on, "Lady Windemere is quite regretful she is not here to pay our neighbors respect today."

The marchioness's eyes gleamed even at this innocuous response.

When finally Hugh stepped forward to bow to Lady Eastley and Alice, he nearly grimaced in anticipation of Miss Winpole's glare. Yet none came. All through the small talk he made with Lady Eastley – yes, the weather had been beautiful; no, he hadn't gone riding; he didn't know yet which ball he'd go to that night – Alice was calm and serene, as she'd been with her other admirers.

"Would you care to see the Fairfax's gardens?" he asked. "If I remember, you have a fondness for reflecting pools, and theirs is quite remarkable."

Miss Winpole glanced to her mother for permission – or perhaps for a save, since Hugh imagined she had no interest in a private walk with him, of all the gentlemen clamoring for her attention. Yet Lady Eastley gave her assent, and so Hugh found himself leading Miss Winpole down the gravel paths of the Fairfax garden.

"Did you enjoy the concert?" he asked, certain that now, away from her mother, Miss Winpole would up-braid him. She had never been too shy to say what was on her mind. At one of the Christmas parties, when they were youngsters spying on the ball, Hugh had asked her to dance, and she'd said "I would never dance with you. You're too tall for me."

He'd seen the anger simmering when his mother warned her away from the duke. Surely that deserved a more scathing rebuke than a ten-year-old's dance request.

"It was beautiful music, wasn't it?" Miss Winpole responded. "I found it quite good for thinking. Which was your favorite movement?"

Hugh had barely noticed the different acts, except to bemoan that he couldn't yet stand. "The third, I suppose."

"That one was very lively. I'd have expected you to

like the second one better. It was more contemplative."

He sifted her words. Was there anger in this observation? Was she trying to insult him, and he was too ignorant of the ways of society to understand it?

He supposed a more practiced gentleman would have a clever enjoinder, and they would merrily continue down the path with as many witticisms as there were blooming crocuses. But Hugh had no patience for this sort of thing. He decided to cut straight to the heart of the matter.

"I wanted to apologize for my mother's remarks the other day. In her usual fashion, she was doing what she felt was best, but I fear it was out of line."

He paused, risking a glance over to his companion to see her reaction so far. Her lips – so rosy, he couldn't help but notice – tightened almost imperceptibly. Hugh took that as a sign that he was not off the mark.

"I have been overindulgent of late with my mother, given her poor health. Still, I knew a little of what she wanted to say before we left for tea, and I regret that I did not try to temper her. We have no place worrying about your Season."

Miss Winpole exhaled, a sweet sigh that reminded him of the swaying trees in the country. "I appreciate your sentiments, Lord Windemere, but surely an apology isn't necessary. My parents and I cherish Lady Windemere as a neighbor and know she has the best of intentions."

How Hugh wished they didn't need to speak between the lines of politeness. "So that wasn't a glimmer of anger in your eyes I saw upon departing?"

They'd come to a Grecian fountain with water leaping from a sculpted goddess's mouth into the awaiting marble basin. Miss Winpole paused, and suddenly Hugh found they were face to face. Her green eyes sparkled up at him. "Surely that isn't a proper question."

Hugh nearly melted into her gaze, lost in the sea of green that was at once playful and dangerous and flirtatious and innocent. He had no words, only the sudden urge to taste her sweet rosy lips.

Miss Winpole turned again, wandering ahead of him on the same path. "You are right, of course. I've been angry with you all week. But the music inspired me to forgiveness. As I said, we cherish you as neighbors, and it is kind of you have such concern for me."

Hugh put one foot in front of the other to follow her. He didn't quite know what was happening, with his heart running at a gallop from one little moment. "I hope you haven't let that anger keep you from enjoying the Season. It seems you've developed a whole club of admirers."

That earned him an impish smile, one which startled him because it brought him so much joy. "It is great fun to have one's dance card fought over. I have you to thank for that, of course. I was a little wallflower before you plucked me for the quadrille. Ever since then, I've barely had a chance to rest."

Hugh's breath caught at the base of his throat. Surely she didn't know the connotations of plucking a flower, or how it conjured fantasies of a wedding night with her on the bed, which was suddenly quite vivid in his mind: Alice in a shimmering nightgown, a full moon illuminating the room, inexplicable flower petals all around her as he…

He cleared his throat. "Glad I could be of service."

"And you? Have you been enjoying the Season? We haven't crossed paths since the marchioness's ball."

"I prefer the company of books," Hugh admitted. "Still, I have promised my mother I will join the Season, perhaps even find a countess before the year is up, so I have resolved to be better and attend more functions."

The words made themselves up as they leapt from his lips. It was everything he *should* be doing, when really the only reason he'd come was to try to convince Miss Winpole to avoid the Duke of Cornwall.

"You're entering the marriage mart?" Miss Winpole smiled playfully. "How exciting. Then we must be friends. I'll help you suffer through the dreadful parts, and you can tell me which of my suitors will make the best husband. Now, describe for me your ideal countess."

This was the opening to warn her again. Instead, his mind blanked. For the life of him, the only ideal countess he could think of was *her*.

Drat if his mother's plan wasn't working.

Chapter Eight

Alice didn't know what had come over her. She'd endeavored to walk with Lord Windemere in the name of forgiveness, with every intention of enjoying the colorful Fairfax flowers more than the conversation.

Instead, she was having almost as good a time as she would have with Lisbeth or Margot.

She might even be *flirting*.

With Lord Windemere.

It was fortuitous that he'd introduced such a topic as a future countess to steer them to safer territory. All she needed to do was convince him they were mere friends, and this confusing business of getting lost in his eyes could be swept under the rug.

"I'm afraid I don't have in mind a paragon of an ideal countess," he was saying, blue eyes sweeping away toward the sculpted yews.

Alice tsked. "Surely you have *some* preferences. Let's set aside the boring business aspects. Do you care about finding a wife who enjoys reading, as much as you do?"

Lord Windemere looked at her thoughtfully. "Is there such a lady, who would clamor for the next shipment of books?"

"Certainly." Alice wondered what exactly he thought

ladies *did*. "I myself count down the days. What better way to spend a summer afternoon than with a book in the sunshine by the lake?"

"And what kind of books do you partake? Do you read of chemistry, physics, medicine? History? Politics? Or do you prefer the novel?"

He said the last with a hint of disdain, enough that Alice decided not to mention that she was enamored of *Cecilia*. "I assume every lady is different, so you'll need to ask your future countess. My preference at the moment is for history, though I will confess that is partly because my father believes I will scare off a husband if I admit to knowledge of chemistry."

"Is that what you ladies discuss in the drawing room while we have our port? The finer points of chemistry, only to pretend it's been a discussion of embroidery, so the delicate male won't take offense upon entering?"

She smirked at him. "I would hate to offend your male sensibility by illuminating you as to what goes on in the drawing room."

There she went again, getting lost in the piercing blue of his eyes as he smiled back at her. Alice hadn't realized Lord Windemere could be funny, or take a joke, or even handle a non-serious conversation. She felt like she had discovered a whole new person, all by choosing to forgive him.

Realizing she'd been staring too long, Alice broke away, carrying down the path a few steps ahead of him.

"Now, your future countess must read books. What else? Do you care for her to be musically accomplished?"

Lord Windemere caught up to walk by her side. "How accomplished would you say the average debutante is this Season?"

Alice hadn't the slightest idea. "Any well-bred lady can play a few songs. I myself have a repertoire of perhaps ten, but no more, since my family prefers games or plays or reading over music as entertainment."

"I have always admired your family for how you enjoy each other's company. I enjoy a good game much more than sitting in a stiff chair listening to a performance."

There was a loneliness behind his first statement that reminded Alice of the lost siblings. Throughout her childhood, there'd been birth announcements down at Richmond Hall, as often as there was news that another child had died. She'd met one or two of Hugh's siblings, a little Emma who was three and Penelope who was five, but they'd both been taken by a fever before Hugh had turned ten. The others had either died before Alice was born or didn't make it out of infancy. It was only when his father died, too – when Hugh was ten – that the news from Richmond Hall stopped.

She clung to his second sentence, therefore, to avoid an impolite acknowledgment of grief. "Fine, then we don't need to worry about finding a musical young lady for you. She must like books and games. What else adds up to your ideal countess?"

So wrapped up in the quiz, Alice hadn't heard any footsteps approaching. Now she jumped when a new voice interrupted. "Already playing the marriage mama, Miss Winpole?"

Alice didn't need to turn around to see who it was. Just the deep timbre sent a delectable shiver down her spine. The Duke of Cornwall, returned at last.

She stepped backward to greet him, putting on her most brilliant smile. There he was, taller than she remembered. Stronger than she remembered. His small coat was cut just so, to highlight his trim waist and boastful chest. His eyes spooled dark secrets as he bowed, keeping her in his sights the whole time. Alice could barely breathe for being in his presence.

"Your Grace, what a delightful surprise." She swept into a curtsy.

"The delight is all mine. The heavenly Lady Eastley directed me to find you here and escort you back, as she said you simply must try the cream eclairs Lady Fairfax has just put out."

"We were about to turn back," Lord Windemere said. Alice had nearly forgotten he was there. Now she saw his face had turned to stone, that somber expression of his frozen into his eyes.

"Lord Windemere was kind enough to show me the reflecting pool." Though they never had quite found it, had they? She batted her eyes to Lord Windemere, hoping in one fell swoop to beg upon their new friendship and remind him how angry she had been when he interfered before. "You don't mind, my lord? I do love an éclair."

He didn't meet her eyes. He merely nodded once, a bow of the head really, and stepped back, almost into the bed of lavender.

"Excellent. Most sporting of you, Osborne." The duke slapped Lord Windemere on the shoulder, then turned on his heel toward the house. He offered his arm to Alice. Custom dictated that she wouldn't take it, being an unmarried lady, but he was a duke, and he was magnetic. She barely thought as she placed her hand upon his forearm.

And promptly lost her breath again.

"I have been neglecting you," the duke started. "After our fateful dance, I had to retire to the country for the week to see to a few matters. Imagine my dismay to return and find I am no longer at the top of your dance card. In fact, it seems you'll need multiple dance cards just to entertain all the suitors you've earned yourself."

Alice tried to laugh, though it came out as a nervous titter. "You flatter me, Your Grace, though I suspect even your exaggeration is exaggerated. Lord Windemere, for example, is merely a family friend kind enough to take me out for some air."

The duke stopped, turning her to face him. They were back near the Grecian fountain, only this time in a corner by the yews. There was no line of sight to the salon; nor was there anyone else around. They were all alone.

"In the Season, Miss Winpole, there is no such thing

as a mere friend."

He said it so intensely, his voice felt as if it were sinking straight into her heart. Somehow, he'd claimed her hands, as well, holding them tight and close. Alice could see the stubble darkening his sharp jaw. She could smell peppermint on his breath. If she reached up, she could outline his lips with her finger.

She could kiss him.

"Forgive my tone," he said. "It is only that I've never quite felt the way I do now, at your side. May I speak candidly?"

Alice nodded.

"Ever since I got back from the West Indies, I've been surrounded by the worst people. They only care for my station, or for what I can do for them. They want to breathe my air, but they suffocate me.

"Yet you – lovely Miss Winpole – you restore me. It is as if you can see straight through my defenses. With only a few words, you understand my heart."

She hadn't thought it could be true. Even as Alice had spent her evenings dreaming of dancing with the duke again, predicting what would make him smile, what would make him stare, what would make him bare his soul, she'd told herself she couldn't possibly know how the duke would react. They'd only barely met.

But here was proof that they hadn't needed more than that one dance to match spirits.

"You are above the *ton*," she responded. "They don't

know how to respond to your glory, so they smother you. They don't understand your soul is too big to be captured in their meager conversation."

"You see? You make me forget myself," the duke murmured, not moving. "I've never been quite so overcome."

This was the man who had spent two years in the West Indies, who was the hoped-for husband of all of London. And he'd never been quite so overcome as he was *by her*. Alice was saving her first kiss for her husband. But the duke stole the words from her, and she forgot herself. She forgot everything except a desperate, wonderful need to be kissed. To have him wrap her close against him and lay waste to her.

"Your Grace," she managed to say, though she didn't know where she was going with that. His finger flew to her mouth, the rough seam of his glove pressing into her lip. It might as well have pressed through the seam of her body, so quickly it heated her tongue, her breasts, her belly. She moved her free hand to his lapel, grasping for life, pulling him even closer. How she wanted to kiss him.

But he stepped away. The storm in his eyes cleared. They were no longer touching, and Alice had never been quite so desolate.

"Call me Alan," the duke said. "At the very least, we can do that."

"As you wish, Alan." It came out almost as a whimper. He smiled.

"Let us see to that éclair."

Chapter Nine

"I love you, Alan. I miss you, Alan. Come here and kiss me, Alan."

"Oh, do shut up!" Alice hissed at Lisbeth, but she couldn't put much meanness behind it. She was simply too giddy.

"Tell me the story again," Lisbeth demanded.

They were sheltering for the afternoon away from the *ton* and the rain at Lisbeth's house, which at Frampton Square was much more fashionable than the Winpole's home in Humphrey Park. Lady Eastley and Lady Ipswich were taking tea in the drawing room while Lisbeth had squirreled Alice away to the library for a bit of catching up.

It had only been a day since the fateful walk in the Fairfax gardens, and Alice already felt as if it had been a lifetime. She was a changed person, now that she had been touched by the duke. By Alan.

"Don't be silly. You could recite it by heart by now." They'd collapsed on the leather chairs by the fire as Alice first told Lisbeth how the duke had claimed her from Lord Windemere, how he'd confessed his jealousy, how they'd so nearly kissed.

She'd been bursting at the seams to tell Lisbeth. Alice knew better than to confess such a transgression to her parents – even to Margot – though she had reported to her parents that the duke had said sweet nothings on the walk. But if she told them of how she'd nearly melted out of her skirts, Lady Eastley would stay by her side every last moment of the Season until Alice was actually married.

Alice sauntered over to the bookshelves. Lord Ipswich was famous for his library, which took the place of their ballroom and featured wall-to-wall bookshelves, glorious reading chaise lounges, and three fireplaces. Alice examined the titles in search of the novel they were supposedly fetching: *The Sylph* by the infamous Duchess of Cavendish. All she saw were gold-lettered titles on Euclidean geometry, Greek philosophy, Newtonian math. Lord Windemere popped to mind. Would he really not mind a countess who worked her way through such concepts?

"Surely the duke will offer for your hand soon," Lisbeth said. "Are you prepared to become a duchess?"

"Of course. I've been practicing my snobby look all morning." Alice looked down her nose at Lisbeth in her best impression of Lady Windemere, who wasn't a duchess but certainly acted like one.

Oh, was she ready to become a duchess. More specifically, she was ready to become the duke – Alan's – duchess. The thrill of walking into a ball with him, knowing she was the one he'd chosen. The secret looks he'd give her as they suffered sycophants, one dark gaze enough to whisper he'd prefer to be alone with her. And when they were alone…she shivered in delight when she let her mind go past the point of decency, to imagine the duke – *Alan* – dipping down to kiss her, hands burning trails wherever he touched. Alice didn't quite know what happened on a wedding night, but she knew it would be delicious.

"I'm shriveling as we speak," Lisbeth giggled. Then she sighed. "Oh, you're having all the fun. The Duke of Cornwall pining over you, flowers from the Earl of Thorne, and of course the Earl of Windemere making moon eyes at you. Meanwhile, all I have is old and ugly Mr. Lansdell clamoring for a chance at *my* dowry."

"He's not that ugly," Alice protested, though it was hard to find Mr. Lansdell's virtues when one had to look at his shaggy silver eyebrows all night. "And the Earl of Windemere is not making moon eyes at me. He's simply a friend."

"A friend who was walking you through the Fairfax gardens. Much like the duke did subsequently, which led to the infamous Alan episode."

Alice pulled out a book of chemistry and pretended to study it. "We were having a very *friendly* discussion about his mother's health and his future countess. The latter of which, by the way, we very much agreed would not be me. I'm merely helping him determine which lady would suit him best."

"How about me?" Lisbeth popped out of her seat, joining Alice at the shelves.

"Why would you want to marry the Earl of Windemere? You'd have to move to the north, and all he does is invent things. You'd be bored silly."

"Not true. I'm a learned woman. I'm sure I'd find the conversation stimulating. Besides, I think Lord Windemere is handsome, even if you don't. There's something thrilling about those spectacles."

Alice scoffed. She thought she'd been the only one to notice how nicely his spectacles sat on his face. "I never said he isn't handsome."

"And he doesn't have gallons of gambling debt, nor does he have a horde of children, nor is he already infamous for keeping three mistresses."

The first referred to the Earl of Thorne; the second to the Marquess of Asbury; the third Alice didn't know. She leaned in conspiratorially. "Which gentleman has three mistresses?"

Lisbeth grinned, wickedness spreading across her face as she realized she knew something Alice didn't. "I'm not telling until you promise to put in a good word for me with the Earl of Windemere. Unless, that is, you want him over *Alan*."

The game of it all disappeared. Alice should want to help her friend, and Lord Windemere and Lisbeth would likely get on famously. Yet the thought of pushing them towards each other turned her stomach.

"You're setting your sights too low, Miss Lisbeth. I promise to help you find the perfect match, rather than settle for the Earl of Windemere just because you think he's handsome."

Lisbeth's eyes narrowed. She was surely about to call Alice's bluff when the door on the far side of the library opened, presenting Lord Windemere himself.

Catching sight of them, he coughed. "Do excuse me, ladies. I'm just stopping by to borrow a few titles from Lord Ipswich."

Lisbeth smiled serenely. "Certainly. May I be of service? It is sometimes quite daunting to find the book you're searching for."

He stepped closer. His hair was wet from the rain, which meant it lay heavier against his face, drawing a better outline of his broad forehead and noble cheekbones. "Thank you. Could you point me toward the steam engine? Or perhaps any section on mechanics, to get started."

"Why that's right here." Lisbeth was perhaps disappointed they happened to be standing not a foot from the correct shelf. She added extra coquettishness to her helpful point. "Are you playing the inventor again, Lord Windemere?"

He wore that somber expression that he was so fond of, the one that made it seem he didn't have the slightest sense of humor. Alice wondered what he was thinking beneath it. Perhaps secretly he had a wicked rejoinder, and he was simply too reserved to say it.

"Miss Dawes, I wouldn't dare do something so un-gentlemanly," Lord Windemere said. "I'm simply reading up on the material."

"I should love to hear more about what you learn." It was awfully forward of Lisbeth to say. Alice nearly gasped. She supposed Lisbeth was trying to make a point to *her,* but it cast her as a little desperate to Lord Windemere. He glanced between them, as if Alice could help him decipher the correct response. Then he bowed, ever so slightly, to Lisbeth and retreated to his bookshelf.

"We should be getting back to tea," Alice said to Lisbeth. "Our mamas will worry we've fallen into the fire."

Lisbeth sighed. "I suppose you're right." From the shelf nearest the door, she retrieved *The Sylph,* so as to keep up their farce, then led Alice back into the corridor. Once the door closed, she turned another one of her amused smiles onto Alice. "If you aren't sweet on Lord Windemere, why did you tear me away so quickly?"

"I didn't tear you away. We were two unmarried ladies alone in a room with an unmarried man. Common sense dictates it was time for us to go."

"Whatever you say, my dear Miss Winpole." Lisbeth glanced down to Alice's hands. "Why are you still holding onto that book? Are you planning on wooing *Alan* with chemistry?"

Alice had forgotten she carried it. "I suppose I'd better go put it back."

"Common sense would dictate it, lest our mamas think you're trying to make yourself unmarriageable. I'll meet you in the drawing room."

They parted ways with one last smirk from Lisbeth. Alice hurried back to the library, not forgetting for one instant that she was returning to Lord Windemere.

Chapter Ten

There were few places Hugh loved more than Lord Ipswich's library. One day, when he was pressed to spend more time in London, he hoped to similarly convert his own ballroom into a library, though his might also include an indecent worktable so he could try out some of the concepts while reading them. In the meantime, Dawes had invited him to visit his Frampton Square oasis at Hugh's leisure.

He'd come for one book, a little red-leather volume he'd seen previously that was all about the steam powered engine. But as usual, he was lost in the shelves again, fingering each spine, fluttering open pages, falling into a chapter before remembering he didn't have time to learn about carriage wheels at the moment.

He was in the midst of the autobiography of Benjamin Franklin, to whom Hugh was indebted for the bifocal spectacle, when the library door opened again. Hugh looked up from his crouch near the bottom of the shelf – Lord Ipswich felt the American authors belonged closest to the dirt – expecting a footman or Lord Ipswich himself. But of course, it wasn't anyone within realm of reason. It was Miss Alice Winpole, back to torture his heart.

She was so comfortably beautiful in her simple periwinkle dress. After their conversation at Fairfax, he'd been inspired to, instead of sleeping, tear through his meager poetry collection in search of the right words to describe her. Angelic, from afar. Cherubic, when she smiled. Goddess-like, when she set her hazy green eyes on him.

The poetry hadn't worked out. Words fumbled across the page like stones damming a stream. He threw the parchment into the fire lest the servants find it. Even they, who could barely read, would find it laughable.

He'd tried writing a letter, too, this one less to confess his love and more to warn her off the duke. How his stomach had turned, to see her take Cornwall's arm. She'd beamed so happily, as if she were the luckiest girl in the world. Hugh had seen how the duke toyed with her, tucked her away into the yews for just so long. Anyone who knew the duke at all could see it was a sham, but Miss Winpole didn't know him. She believed he was lost in her eyes.

The letter had ended up in the fire, too.

"I forgot to put back this book before leaving," Miss Winpole confessed, startling Hugh from his reverie. "Perhaps you want it."

She stepped close enough for Hugh to see the freckles sprinkled across her nose and cheeks and forehead. He'd forgotten them; likely at all the other events, she'd had them covered with powder.

He took the book, since she held it out for him. It was the old Antoine Lavoisier classic on chemistry. Hugh couldn't help but smile. "A debutante who reads chemistry? I do believe you'll lose your dancing privileges over this."

Miss Winpole's eyes widened as she laughed, as if she shared his shock that he'd make a joke. "It's quite indecent. Why, you might have to offer for me out of honor if we were caught discussing the book."

She was teasing, but her words shot through Hugh as if she'd stripped off her dress. To be caught together – oh, how he'd love to kiss her indecently. To offer for her. Somewhere between the letter and the poetry and the not sleeping, Hugh had admitted to himself he just might be in love with Miss Winpole. Beautiful Miss Winpole. Smart Miss Winpole. Funny Miss Winpole. She was warm and witty and would undoubtedly fill his lonely life with games and children and toasty afternoons by the fire.

But she was only teasing.

"It would be the scandal of the summer," Hugh heard himself say, though he didn't know where he found the wit.

Alice's eyes traced across his face. "Do you not use an umbrella?"

He blinked at the non-sequitur. His hand flew to his head quite unconsciously and discovered his hair was, indeed, still damp from the rain. Hugh blushed. "I'm afraid you've caught me, Miss Winpole. I stepped out with the intention of only running to the back of my garden, where

I keep a few extra books, but I got carried away. To here, specifically. I suppose I look unsuitably disheveled."

"Disheveled, yes." Alice's gaze softened into his. Hugh felt his world shrink; nothing existed except for her. "I wouldn't say unsuitable. The effect is rather handsome."

He had never before felt quite this light. He didn't think it was scientifically possible to float off, but Hugh's whole body felt as if he were suspended in the air. He tried to memorize this moment. Even if he never spoke to Miss Winpole again, he could have this specific instant to remember for always.

And then, inexplicably, she touched him. She raised a perfect finger to his hair and brushed it from his temple to behind his ear. Hugh couldn't breathe. He caught her hand in his palm, holding it there against his ear. He could hear a heartbeat, racing.

And he wondered if he should kiss her. They were close, breathing the same air. All it would take was a small step forward, a little bend at the neck. Heaven, just a chance away. She was touching him. Did she want him to kiss her?

Hugh was about to take the risk when the moment ended. Alice blinked, as if she'd been in a trance, and jumped backward. Her hand fled his touch.

"I do apologize," she said, breathlessly. "There was a curl..."

She blushed a ferocious red, all the way past the

neckline of her dress. Hugh hated to see her discomfort. He turned away, toward the shelves, to signal he was no danger to her. "You are, as ever, a good friend."

"I'd better get back to tea." Alice – Miss Winpole, he reminded himself – fled for the door. Hugh watched her go from the corner of his eye, too lost to understand what had happened.

It was only eons later, when he was still staring blankly at the shelves, that he realized he hadn't warned her off the Duke of Cornwall.

Chapter Eleven

The Countess of Pemberly's ball would be the most extravagant of the Season yet, so it was a Winpole family affair to attend. Margot, whose husband had returned to the country for a week, left her children asleep and arrived just after tea to be coiffed alongside Alice. Lady Eastley changed gowns three times. Lord Eastley had to wait for an hour in his smoking room before the ladies declared themselves ready to depart.

"I have that feeling in my elbow that tells me this night will be momentous," Lord Eastley declared in the carriage. "Same as the night dear old Geoff arrived to Bleneccle Manor. That can only mean one thing: you'll get an offer tonight, Alice."

Margot squealed on behalf of Alice, who was too excited to emote. She wore her favorite gown of all, a peach-colored organza that drifted dreamily across her body, and Lady Eastley had loaned her a beautiful string of pearls. Even her hair shone with diamond-studded pins. It was her most sophisticated look yet.

Perfect for a future duchess.

The Duke of Cornwall had sent her flowers that morning, with a note saying he looked forward to dancing the supper waltz with her.

So too had the Earl of Thorne and the Marquess of

Asbury, but the former was the one that had sent the household into a tizzy.

"Should she dance with others to be coy?" Lady Eastley asked Lord Eastley. "Or should she be at the disposal of the duke all night?"

"He is likely to arrive later," Lord Eastley declared. "Let him see that she is coveted. It will induce him to show his hand more quickly. But if you have promised a dance to one gentleman and the duke requests to step in – by all means, let him step in."

Alice looked to Margot for a reality check. When they'd packed up Bleneccle Manor for the trip down to London, Alice's wildest dreams had included falling in love with a dashing marquess. She hadn't even thought she might win a duke's heart.

Margot waggled her eyebrows at Alice obligingly. "You won't forget us common folk once you've joined the duchy, will you old Al?"

"Certainly not, though your visits will of course be limited, so as not to embarrass my new family."

"Embarrass? Me? I'm not the one who once caught her head feathers on fire." Margot directed this toward their mother, who had famously caught flame at one of the parties during her Season.

Lady Eastley smiled indulgently. "However, you are the one who jumped into the lake wearing nothing but her chemise at the wise age of sixteen."

The carriage arrived to the Pemberly house. Though

the sun had long since set, the place was ablaze with the orange glow of candlelight. A footman rushed to help the ladies down: first Lady Eastley, then Margot, and finally Alice.

"Isn't this everything?" Margot sighed, wrapping an arm through Alice's. "You are living the dream. How proud I am to be your sister."

"Stop with that gushing. You're making me nervous."

The ball was already in full swing when they were announced. The Countess of Pemberly complimented their outfits and pointed them toward the refreshment tables. "I believe one or two of your admirers are already awaiting you," she whispered to Alice.

Indeed, the Earl of Thorne rushed to her side, claiming the first quadrille. His smile was full of yellowed teeth, and Alice felt a rush of gratitude that soon, she wouldn't need to humor him anymore.

She used the dance to scan the crowd. There was no sign of the Duke of Cornwall, though of course he could have hidden himself in the card room until the supper waltz. Lisbeth was there, dancing with the Marquess of Asbury, and Margot had accepted a turn with Mr. Lansdell, a great act of charity for all the debutantes.

It was just as the quadrille came to a close that Alice noticed Lord Windemere. He stood by the refreshment table, looking uncomfortable as the Marchioness of Leighster chatted at him. Alice wondered if the marchioness was telling tales or trying to get new ones out of Hugh.

Certainly he wouldn't say a word about the library.

It had been three days since that strange moment. Alice had mostly succeeded in not thinking about it, steering her fantasies to the duke – Alan – every time Hugh popped into her mind. She still couldn't say what had possessed her to touch him, other than that one rain-splattered strand was stubbornly curling into a fly-wheel. Her hand had acted on its own. And how startlingly soft Hugh's hair had been. How kind his eyes, as they widened in surprise. How sweet his hand, as it pressed her close.

All things considered, Alice decided it would be better to avoid Lord Windemere until she was safely engaged to the Duke of Cornwall.

Which was why she was more than a little dismayed when he approached on Lady Eastley's arm for the minuet preceding the supper waltz.

"You need a partner for this one, don't you, Alice?" her mother said, an instruction if ever there was one.

She curtsied to Lord Windemere, trying her hardest not to look at his face. Alice didn't want to see his eyes. She followed him to their spot on the dance floor, crushed between the other dancers.

"How goes your search for a countess?" she asked, an attempt to keep the conversation on neutral territory.

"Slowly, I'm afraid." Hugh's voice was soft in the din of the room. Alice had to strain to hear him, which meant she drew closer to him. And inhaled his tantalizingly spicy scent. "I'm a poor mixture of shy and picky."

Alice opened her mouth to offer to make some introductions for him. Instead, she said, "The right countess will be able to see through that to your true charisma."

Hugh smiled; she could see it out of the corner of her eye. "And what of you? I told you about my ideal countess. What is your ideal husband?"

They separated to sashay down the line of dancers. When they rejoined at the bottom of the line, Alice responded, "I came to the Season with the usual stipulations. A gentleman of good breeding, handsome to look at, who will cherish me as a wife and whom I can cherish. Now my ideal is more particular. Namely, there is one gentleman in particular."

Lord Windemere had her hand to lead through the dance. His grip tightened. Too keenly, she suddenly remembered that moment in the library, when she had nearly thrown herself at him to be held.

"I think I know that gentleman. At the risk of earning your wrath again, Miss Winpole, I feel, as a friend, I must say something before you lose more than your heart to the Duke of Cornwall."

Alice nearly stopped dancing. The nerve of him, to say something so searingly personal on the dance floor. "Lord Windemere, I believe we have covered this territory. Your mother's fears are unfounded."

"The Duke of Cornwall is more than your ordinary rake. I know him from school, more than I'd like to know.

He is a tormentor and a bully, and I do not believe his interest in you is wholesome, honest, nor based in admiration. In fact, I have reason to believe he is dallying with you only to extend his longstanding torment of me."

The minuet was coming to a close, and Lord Windemere whispered his words so urgently, he sounded like a steaming teapot.

Alice could barely manage the curtsy demanded by the dance. She raised her eyes to level Hugh with the greatest glare she could muster. "The nerve you have, to make an honorable marriage suit into something so twisted, when you cannot muster the courage to even speak to young ladies. I pity you, Lord Windemere. And now I must ask that you keep your person and your opinions away from me for the rest of the evening."

She whirled around, barely able to see where she was going. Her hands shook in anger. To think she'd flirted with Lord Windemere. That she'd called him handsome. When really he was so narcissistic to think the Duke of Cornwall was paying her attention as some sick vendetta against Lord Windemere. The man who inspired passion in exactly zero people? The idea was absurd.

Alice was so flustered, she forgot all about the supper waltz. The Duke of Cornwall found her by the refreshment table, glaring at the fleur-de-lis wallpaper.

"My dear Miss Winpole, whatever is the matter? You look as angry as Napoleon himself upon defeat."

Tears pricked Alice's eyes, though she couldn't say

whether they were from anger or gratitude that Alan cared. "I do apologize. My latest dance partner has flustered me."

The duke surveyed the crowd with his dark eyes, a protective anger hardening his looks into that of a general. "The Earl of Windemere? If you pardon my boldness, that man has been a disgrace since he first arrived at Eton. He was always too full of himself, just because he was made earl at the age of ten. I shouldn't take anything he says to heart."

Alice's heart flinched at the word *disgrace*. But clearly, there was no love lost between Lord Windemere and Alan, and if she had to place her bets on one of them, she'd choose the one lauded as the catch of London, not the gentleman who spent his spare time secretly hunched over his worktable like a commoner.

"A dance hardly seems appropriate given your disposition at the moment. Perhaps I can lighten your mood with a turn through the gardens?"

Alice glanced at her parents, who were watching the conversation from their little circle near the entrance. Lord Eastley nodded encouragingly. Though he couldn't possibly know the duke had proposed a slightly risqué walk, Alice understood the message: humor His Grace. After all, this could be the walk during which the duke asked for her hand.

"You know exactly how to speak to my heart," Alice said, mustering up a charming smile. "Lead the way."

The gardens were not empty, by any means. A cluster of gentlemen smoked cigars on the patio, and couples flirted discreetly against the marble column fence. As the duke led Alice down the stairs into the paths of flower beds, candelabras illuminated friends chatting and more couples catching some alone time.

"Tell me more about the West Indies," Alice said. "Are they very different from here?"

"Very. The weather is always warm, hotter than summer. The water is so bright it blinds. The buildings don't have doors or windows so that the breeze can run through."

Alice blushed at the thought of a house without a door. "Do you miss it?"

"May I tell you a secret?" Alan ran his dark eyes over Alice, then smiled to himself. "Of course I may. You're my Alice."

His hand brushed against hers with the words, and she nearly tripped, so lost in the thrumming of her heart.

"I burn with anger that I had to leave. I was responsible for keeping an entire city safe. Men and women alike turned to me as their leader. How can running ducal estates compare to that?"

Anger shone through his voice, too, thickening it until Alice barely recognized it. A tiny part of her shivered, as if she were in danger.

She took Alan's hand. As glad as she was he had returned to London, she hated to hear he was miserable.

"Why did you have to leave?"

For a long moment, she didn't think he would answer. Alan stared ahead of them, as if he were funneling his response into the silent dark.

But he did respond. "There is much about my life you couldn't understand."

Alice, still holding his hand, tugged him to a stop. "I am your Alice. I was born to understand."

Taking her in, he smiled, erasing the dark brood from his face. "You are my Alice, aren't you? The moonlight becomes you. You are particularly beautiful this evening."

As much as she wished he'd make her his confidante, Alice understood the end of a subject. She returned his smile with her own. "And you, Your Grace, are the most dashing gentleman at the ball."

"I thought I told you to call me Alan. I want to hear it from your lips."

"Alan." She blushed as she said it.

His hand brushed her cheekbone. Quite suddenly, Alice realized they'd meandered to a secluded part of the garden, where the candles didn't quite illuminate the hedges. Where there were no other people about.

It was just like at the Fairfax garden, only this time, he might actually kiss her.

Or she might kiss him.

She smiled at his touch. Dared to put her hand on his cheek, almost as she had done in the library with Lord Windemere. Alan's face was sharper against her fingers from his stubble. She couldn't make out his eyes in the darkness. Couldn't see if he was ravishing her with looks alone.

All she could do was feel.

And oh, how she felt, when he did swoop in for that first kiss, that long, heady, wonderful, sensual first kiss.

Chapter Twelve

Hugh couldn't have felt worse if she'd slapped him. In fact, it would have been better if she had slapped him. The physical sting would at least fade away.

The sting of her words, however, would stay with him the rest of his lifetime.

He staggered away from their minuet in a blind, deaf daze. *I must ask you to keep your person and your opinions away from me.*

He'd bungled it, that was for sure. His only goal had been to make her see the duke with wide open eyes. To understand that behind Cornwall's pretty words lurked a darker motivation.

Instead, he'd driven her further into the duke's arms.

There was no use staying longer. He had no interest in playing cards with Lord Eastley or nodding with Lady Eastley while Alice whirled around with Alan the Snake. That she had declared herself set on the duke was painful enough to hear; that she wanted nothing to do with Hugh was worse.

Hugh was on his way out when Lady Phoebe, the Marchioness of Leighster, intercepted him. "My dear Lord Windemere, I am feeling faint. Won't you take me to the garden for a breath of fresh air?"

There was no polite way to decline, so Hugh found himself emerging from his daze under the starlight in the company of the Matron of Society.

"Your mother told me how she wishes you would find a wife this Season," the Marchioness said, though Hugh could have sworn they'd already had this conversation. "Have you set your sights on anyone? I noticed you dancing with Miss Winpole."

Hugh's heart hammered all over again. Must everyone notice everything? Would the disastrous minuet be thrown into his face every time he turned around, for the rest of his life?

"Miss Winpole and I remain friends from growing up as neighbors, but I daresay she has higher designs than me." Hugh could hear the bitterness in his words. He tried to swallow it back. "She has been most kind to offer to help introduce me to other young ladies of her set who might be appropriate as Countess of Windemere."

"Indeed?" The marchioness lifted her diamond-encrusted lorgnette as if to examine Hugh's statement. Then she swung around, lifting her regal arm towards a couple just entering the marble patio. "Ho, Lord and Lady Eastley!"

Hugh cringed. After everything, the last thing he wanted was to speak to Alice's parents. Suppose Alice told them about the library, or worse, shared his words from the minuet after the ball. They'd never so much as look at him again.

"Lord Windemere was just taking me for a turn. Won't you join us? There are the most exquisite white lilies in this garden."

How Hugh wished he could end this blasted evening. Instead, he obligingly escorted the marchioness through the garden, all the while listening to the easy chitchat of the ladies sharing thoughts on designing the perfect flower bed. Every now and then, Lord Eastley weighed in with his heavy chuckle: "Don't ask me to tell a rose and carnation apart," or "The most beautiful flower is, of course, my wife."

"The lilies are just over here," Lady Leighster said, freeing Hugh of her grip so she could take a candelabra from its stand and lead the group to the furthest northwest corner. Hugh hung back, ostensibly to let Lady Eastley see the lilies better. But instead of illuminating flowers, the candle lit upon a couple in the hedges.

A quite indecent couple. Kissing ferociously. The lady's skirt hiked well past her knee. The gentleman's hand dangerously close to her bosom. And whimpers of pleasure, interrupted abruptly by the light.

"Now see here!" the marchioness gasped. "What kind of behavior is this?"

The gentleman took a languorous step to the side, while the lady jumped away with a squeal of embarrassment. And even in the candlelight, it was plain as day who they were: none other than Miss Winpole and the Duke of Cornwall.

Hugh's heart may have stopped for a beat. He wanted to disappear. Evaporate faster than steam from hot water.

"My lord, my lady. Marchioness." The duke nodded at all of them, as if they were encountering each other on an everyday promenade. For Hugh, his lips slithered into a smirk. "Windemere."

"It seems you got carried away, eh, Cornwall?" Lord Eastley said, a trace of humor in his tone.

Hugh felt sick to his stomach as Cornwall responded. "Indeed, Lord Eastley."

"There's an easy fix to that, isn't there?" Lord Eastley now looked to the marchioness, as if this were all a joke.

"What would that be?" The duke had a polite veneer to his sneer, but a sneer it still was.

"Why, marriage, of course." For the first time, Lord Eastley didn't sound as if he were laughing. In the candlelight, Alice looked to the duke, her eyes wide and bright with expectation.

But the duke only withdrew a handkerchief and wiped his lips. As if Alice had sullied them. "My dear Lord Eastley, if you think I'm interested in being trapped into matrimony by a young lady who throws herself at me, you are sorely mistaken. I am a duke. I have some standards for my future duchess."

To her credit, Alice's face didn't crumple. She didn't wail, nor did she faint. She simply stared at the man she held in such high esteem.

Hugh's heart broke all over again.

"Your Grace, I'm afraid it's too late for that," the marchioness said. "You have been *discovered*. The scandal that would erupt if you didn't offer for Miss Winpole... she would be cut from Society in disgrace."

The duke set his cold eyes on Alice, then looked back to the marchioness. "A disgrace she well deserves, don't you think?"

Lady Eastley gasped. Lord Eastley charged forward, nearly taking the duke by the lapels. "You disgraced her. You will marry her. It is the honorable thing to do."

The duke stepped past Lord Eastley. "My lord, if you only knew me, you would understand that honor does not compel me. Nothing, in fact, compels me. I do what I want, when I want it."

"You are a peer of this land, and you are bound by the same laws of honor as the rest of us. I will have satisfaction."

"Then I will kill you." The duke stared down at Lord Eastley, the same glare that used to incite fear in Hugh the minute he walked into a room. Alice cried out, a wordless sob.

The duke loped off, a gentlemanly stride despite everything. Hugh could have put out a hand and stopped him, but what good would it do? Cornwall had accomplished his goal. He had ruined Miss Winpole, all because she was dear to Hugh.

"If his mother were alive to see him behave like

this..." the marchioness muttered. "What a scandal. What a to-do."

As if for the first time, Lady Eastley seemed to realize that none other than society's biggest gossip had witnessed the whole scene. "Lady Leighster, you won't tell anyone, will you? This can stay in the family, so to speak."

"How could it stay in the family?" The marchioness looked at Lady Eastley as if she had sprouted two heads. "The girl is no suitable prospect for any gentleman. No one will offer for her now."

"Give us just a few days," Lord Eastley said, desperation lacing his words now. "I will bring the duke to his senses."

Lady Leighster shook her head sadly. "You had better. For if he doesn't marry her, who will?"

And for the first time, perhaps in his entire life, Hugh knew it was his time to act. There was no indecision, no quivering over whether anyone else wanted him to do it. His heart compelled him forward.

"I will."

Chapter Thirteen

When Alice's maid drew back the bedroom curtains, the morning light was so perfect that for a moment, Alice didn't remember what had happened. She thought she was cozied in bed back at Bleneccle Manor where the sun shone bright and strong more than once in a blue moon. She stretched her arms, plotting in her half-sleep to take her mare for an extra-long ride around the lake.

Then she heard the clatter of wagon wheels on cobblestone, mixed with the sing-song wails of a muffin man hauling wares, and she remembered.

She was in London.

She was disgraced.

She was marrying Lord Hugh Osborne, Earl of Windemere.

Alice curled back under her covers, biting back a moan. She didn't know how she had gone from anticipating the duke's offer to shuttling through the back door into her parents' coach. He had told her to call him Alan — that wasn't something one did unless one meant to make an offer. He had steered her into the gardens, a place one didn't venture with a debutante if one was just trifling. He had told her his secrets.

And *he* had been the one to kiss her. Alice tingled all

over again remembering how he had devoured her. She'd known it was wrong. She'd known she should stop him, even as she had laced her hands around his neck to pull him closer, had pressed her body flush against his, had made space as his palm mapped the territory from her chin down her neck to her bosom.

She'd known it was shameful. She'd known they should wait at least until an offer was in place. But it was clear as the country morning sun that she hadn't been trying to trap him. She was following his lead.

So why was she now engaged to Lord Windemere?

Squeezing her eyes tight, Alice focused on Alan's face. The perfect lines stroked by his eyebrows and cheekbones. The slight misalignment of his nose, from perhaps a fight gone awry in the colonies. His dark, bewitching irises. And his slender lips, which had so passionately explored hers.

There had been a misunderstanding. Alan wanted her. He'd sent her flowers; he'd been eager to dance with her. He'd called her his Alice. Whatever had happened after was simply a matter of one party not understanding the other.

By the time Alice descended to the breakfast room, she was convinced that her father was to blame. Something he'd said upon encountering them – not that she could remember, for she'd been far too horrified to focus on the words flinging around her – had insulted Alan as a duke, and that was why he'd stalked off, leaving her to the mercy of Lord Windemere.

The hour was late – nearly noon – and yet both Lord Eastley and Lady Eastley waited at the table. Usually, when Alice breakfasted with her parents, the room filled with her father's jokes and her mother's laughter, or even with animated conversation. Her parents enjoyed each other's company; on a normal day, one could feel it as soon as one walked into the room.

But that morning, the breakfast table was silent. Lord Eastley perused the newspaper. Lady Eastley, finished with her meal, stirred a spoon through her tea endlessly. When Alice walked in, they both looked up with pasted-on smiles. "How did you sleep, dear?" her mother asked.

"Finally up, eh?" Lord Eastley teased.

Alice squared her shoulders and went directly to the sideboard. She decided to let them lead the conversation for now. It was best to appear the obedient, happy daughter until it was absolutely necessary to fight.

"I believe I was quite exhausted from the excitement of the ball," Alice replied. She fixed a plate of her usual toast, bacon, and soft-boiled eggs, though her stomach was so knotted in anxiety she couldn't imagine eating anything. She took the seat next to her mother, who promptly poured her a cup of tea.

"It's good you rested. The next month will be busy, preparing everything."

"Preparing for what?" Alice tried to open her eyes

innocently as she asked.

Lady Eastley twisted to look her daughter dead-on, as if she'd just asked who was regent or where London was. "For the wedding, of course. Lord Windemere is taking care of the special license, but we've to arrange for announcements, discuss the invitations to the breakfast, set a menu, and there's your trousseau as well."

Hearing his name spoken turned Alice's stomach. In the garden, she'd barely registered his presence. She'd been too horrified at being caught, and still vibrating from the sensations Alan had aroused, to see beyond Alan and her father and the marchioness. It wasn't until that terrible moment when Alan stalked off that she first saw Lord Windemere standing there, just behind Lady Eastley. And then he'd said *that*.

Alice gathered herself with a deep breath. "I'm not marrying Lord Windemere."

The street clatter was suddenly twice as loud, as the breakfast room froze in silence. Alice didn't dare move, didn't dare look at her parents. She stared at the breakfast plate, counting slowly down from one hundred. She was at eighty-one – the lucky year of Alan's birth – when Lady Eastley said, "You must still be overtired, dear. We'll take today off and start preparations tomorrow."

"I'm not overtired." Though her whole body trembled, Alice managed to keep her voice strong and clear. "I'm not marrying Lord Windemere. There was a misunderstanding last night. His Grace expressed every intention of offering for me. We simply must apologize for offending him, and he will offer for me."

Now it was Lord Eastley who spoke, and how Alice hated to hear anything but teasing from her father. She braced, expecting ire, but instead, he sounded weary. "We all thought he intended to offer for you. But he did not. The only misunderstanding was our presumption that the Duke of Cornwall is an honorable peer."

Unbidden, Alice remembered that moment when Alan had looked at her – the only time he looked at her during that whole awful confrontation. *A disgrace she well deserves.*

But before that, before they'd even kissed, he'd said something else: *There is much about my life you couldn't understand.*

"There is some other reason," she said, her voice tearing a little with a sob. "If you'll only let me speak to him again, I'll ease any anxieties he has. He wants to marry me, I know it."

"Your honor has already been impugned. You are never speaking to that man again," her father replied.

"Then *you* go." All hope of keeping her composure gone, Alice hurdled to her father's side, dropping to her knees as if she were still a little girl begging for candy. "Tell him I'm sorry for the scandal. I didn't mean for... what happened...to happen."

"Of course you didn't." Lord Eastley patted her hand. "The duke, on the other hand, knew exactly what he was doing. He invited you to the garden. He...well, if you didn't mean for anything to happen, don't you see that *he* did? For whatever reason, it suited him to use you like some common wench without any intention of doing the honorable thing."

Alice's whole body trembled. Alan had kissed her so passionately. Why would he do it if he didn't mean to offer for her?

I have reason to believe he is dallying with you only to extend his torment of me.

Surely Lord Windemere wasn't right. That was only narcissism. Alan had told her she understood his soul. He'd looked forward to dancing with her. He'd confided his secrets in her.

"It's not right," Alice said. "If you'd only speak to him again. You can straighten this out. I know you can. I love him, Papa."

She'd never said the words, not even in her head. They sounded silly, hanging in the air. Her eyes welled with tears, just hearing them. She was a silly, stupid girl.

"I'd be calling him to task for it, no doubt, Alice my love, if not for Lord Windemere. But don't you see? Right now, the only souls who know about your indiscretion are us, Cornwall, Osborne, and the Marchioness of Leighster. She'll keep quiet as long as Osborne marries you. If I demand satisfaction, you'll be clouded with scandal for the rest of your life. Not to mention, Lord Windemere would not be happy about it. Then you'd be notorious, disgraced, and without a husband."

Alice could barely think of Lord Windemere, could only remember a general fuzz of curly hair and spectacles. He and his mother had taken objection to Alan from the moment the duke set eyes on Alice. Somehow, through dark magic or otherwise, they must have willed this fate on her. "I won't marry him. I won't."

Lady Eastley wrapped an arm around Alice's shoulders, kneeling to join her daughter on the imported silk carpet. "Better a man that wants to marry you than one whose hand is forced. Lord Windemere will make you a fine husband. He is kind, he treats his servants as well as he treats his mother, and he won't worry your heart too much running from one corner of the country to another."

Alice could picture him in a flash now, ten-year-old Hugh sprinting up a great big hill on the Richmond Hall estate to catch his escaped spaniel. She pushed down the memory, for it was filled with the admiration seven-year-old Alice felt for the dashing boy. Somehow, Lord Windemere was the reason she was in this mess, and she wasn't going to feel an ounce of kindness for him.

"Besides," Lady Eastley continued, her voice gentle, "you'll be our neighbor. We can visit each other whenever we want."

It was that moment, the lonely sentiment that Alice would need her mother close to suffer through this marriage, that overwhelmed her. She couldn't form words, or thoughts, or plans. She could only sob, on the floor, in her mother's arms, and feel two things at once.

She would never stop loving Alan, and she would never forgive Lord Windemere.

Chapter Fourteen

Hugh waited until morning to share the news with his mother. After helping the Winpoles escape to their coach out the back of the garden – they were all far too excited to brave the expanse of the ballroom – he'd retreated to his basement workshop. He was but a bundle of emotions. Shock, at what had just transpired. Devastation, to see Alice in the arms of the duke. Humiliation, still, at how she had so efficiently cut him to pieces. And yet a persistent, buoyant happiness.

Miss Alice Winpole was to be his wife.

A night of working at the perfect alignment of gears for his hay cutting machine was supposed to help him think more clearly, but even as he went to bed as dawn broke, Hugh was bewildered as to how he should feel about the strange circumstances of his nuptials.

He decided it was best to be excited.

On the doctor's orders, Lady Windemere had been taking breakfast in her quarters for the past few months, so as not to overexert herself throughout the day. Donning his best morning coat and shiniest shoe buckles, Hugh followed the breakfast tray into his mother's sitting room.

"Care for some company, Mama?"

"What a treat," Lady Windemere exclaimed, the

emotion only reaching her eyes, as usual. She beckoned him to kiss her on the cheek. "You're in a good mood."

"Indeed." Hugh accepted a cup of Assam tea. His mother still prepared it the way he'd liked it as a boy, doctored up with a good gulp of milk and hunk of sugar. These days, he preferred a strong, bitter cup, but he hadn't the heart to share the change with his mother.

"How was the Pemberly ball?" Lady Windemere asked. "If I recall, they have a rather spacious dancing room."

"Yes, it was quite nicely done." He shared with her the refreshments he'd observed and the order of the dances. She loved to hear every detail of the events she missed, so he even tried to describe the more outlandish outfits he'd seen: Lord Henry Greville's maroon-colored coat, Lady Althorpe's nearly transparent dress. "Apparently, the thinnest of cotton is the trajectory of our highest fashion. Perhaps next, ladies will simply show up in their underclothes."

Lady Windemere tsked. "Sometimes, I am grateful to be spared the tedium of seeing such developments. Of course, that's what my grandmother said when I went out in my Season with hair piled three feet high, so perhaps I have no right."

Hugh couldn't imagine his mother as a debutante; it was a sign of his good mood that he took a moment to picture her flitting around a dance room in a skirt five times the circumference of her waist.

"How was the supper? I believe they have a French cook."

Hugh cleared his throat. Here was his favorite and least favorite part of the evening. "I'm afraid I didn't stay to try it."

Lady Windemere skewered him with a mother's glare of disappointment. "I suppose you had a good reason."

"Yes, well." Hugh found himself suddenly without words. He decided to skip all the indecency and cut straight to the heart of the matter. "I am engaged to be married to Miss Alice Winpole."

Lady Windemere's excitement leapt directly to her eyes; it might even have translated into a smile, had it not transformed into a coughing fit. She clutched her handkerchief to her mouth as she hacked, her free hand pressed to her heart.

Hugh so hated to observe these attacks, but just as much, she hated to be fussed over. He stirred his over-sugared tea until she was back to herself.

"Do tell me exactly how this good news came to be, and why it would require you to skip the supper."

And so, Hugh had no saving but to tell her. Skipping over the humiliation of Alice telling him off, he started with the marchioness begging him to walk her through the garden. Rather than describing in detail how Lord Alan's hand had been directly on Alice's shapely rear-end at the moment of discovery, Hugh characterized it as a passionate embrace. He ended, of course, with Lord Eastley accepting his offer of marriage. And through all of it, he kept his eyes on his tea. It was only at the end that he looked up, to see how his mother felt about the news that her plan had worked.

Lady Windemere's expression, as usual, was an unreadable mask. Once Hugh's words had died off, she turned her gaze to the window. "You are marrying a woman in disgrace."

Hugh blinked. "I am marrying Miss Winpole. The young lady you urged me to marry."

"At the time I urged you to marry her, she was very much eligible. At the time you offered for her, she was very much not." Lady Windemere's words were hollow, despite the heat of their meaning. She looked back to Hugh. "I hope you did not offer for her simply because you thought my heart was set on her as your wife."

Hugh could barely make sense of his mother's reaction. Of all the confusion he'd felt since offering for Alice, the one thing he'd counted on was that he had at last truly done something that would please his mother. If he was marrying a woman who didn't love him, at least, he'd reasoned, Lady Windemere would be happy in her last months.

"I did not," Hugh said, not quite hearing his own words. Then his mother kept staring at him, and he realized he needed to be more convincing. Which meant, unfortunately, being more honest. "At the beginning of the

Season, I paid her attention because I knew you wanted me to. In doing so, I discovered I quite care about her. In fact, I went to the ball last night hoping to…well, I suppose I had hoped to capture her attention away from the Duke of Cornwall. Complicated though the situation may be, I am happy about the result."

"And the young lady?" Lady Windemere raised her brow in question. "Is she happy about the result?"

Hugh thought back to his last glimpse of Alice: hair ruffled, dress crumpled, and a tear-streaked face glistening in the moonlight as she huddled against her mother in the coach.

"You must remember, Mama, what we know of Cornwall. She trusted him much as I did in my first year at Eton. I do not find her at fault for succumbing to his strange plots."

"Does she fancy herself in love with him?"

That brought back the sensation of his heart splitting in two, as Alice declared she was interested in one gentleman only.

"I really couldn't say." Hugh put aside his tea, trying to signal the interview was over. "We will be married in a month, so as not to look as if we are trying to cover a scandal. Shall I arrange for you to call on Lord and Lady Winpole?"

Lady Windemere still regarded him with that long, unreadable gaze. Hugh waited, bracing, sure she would say something else that would plummet him into confusion again.

"You have always had such a large heart," she said when she finally spoke. "As a child, you grieved a playmate abandoning you to the same magnitude as a death. I only want someone to protect that heart. I've never been very good at it."

Inexplicably, Hugh thought of his spaniel, Cooper, racing away from him. It was only a few days after his father's funeral, and Hugh had spent the whole week holding tight to Cooper, burying tears in his friend's soft fur. But his visiting cousins spent the same week sneaking bacon to Cooper. When their carriage rolled away, Cooper leapt from Hugh's arms and raced after them. Hugh ran until his lungs gave out, up the hill and down the road and almost to the gates. Eventually, the carriage disappeared. Eventually, Cooper returned, reporting to the kitchen for supper slops. But Hugh never did return to crying.

"I'm overtired today," Lady Windemere said. "I'll send a note to Lady Eastley sharing my felicitations and my intentions to visit tomorrow."

Hugh stood and bowed to his mother. The maid took the cue to remove the breakfast tray while Lady Windemere's personal maid helped her back to bed. Hugh retreated to the hall. He ducked into the guest room, across from his mother's, so the servants couldn't see him. And he sank to the ground, the weight of his mother's implications settling on his shoulders.

In his eagerness, Hugh had imagined that by saving Alice from disgrace, he'd earn her love. Or at least her admiration. But instead, he'd handed her a perfect solution to her problem. A married lady could dally with the duke all she wanted, and no one would bat an eye.

Alice loved the duke. Alice hated Hugh. It wouldn't matter that they were married; it was only a matter of time until she, too, would abandon him.

What had he done?

Chapter Fifteen

Alice couldn't sleep. This time the night before, she'd been on the arm of the Duke of Cornwall, promenading through the garden. Now, she was wrapped in a scratchy counterpane trying to understand why he hadn't offered for her.

Why she still hadn't heard from him.

Why she was so in love with him.

There was a part of her — the calm, rational side that she'd never been fond of — that comprehended that the duke was in the wrong. She was an unmarried lady of peerage; he was an eligible gentleman. By refusing to marry her, the duke threw her into disgrace.

She should condemn him, as everyone else was so eager to do.

But the stronger part of her remembered how Alan made her feel. Kept reliving the memories so she could feel that way over and over again. Seen. Cherished. Trusted.

The problem was that no one else knew Alan as she did. They all saw a cold, unfeeling duke. But Alice had seen beneath that veneer. She'd felt the currents rushing beneath his heart, pulling him backward to the West Indies, carrying him forward to London. He was torn, he was angry, and he trusted no one.

Except her. He trusted her. Enough to tell her his

secrets.

Just not enough to marry her.

It was a math problem Alice could not solve. Yet neither could she stop lining up the different factors – his kiss, his heart, his words – against his actions to try to find the balance.

And so, she tossed, and she turned, and she kept on torturing herself.

The clock was just finishing the last stroke of twelve when Alice heard a rattle against her windowpane. At first, she thought it was merely the patter of rain, but then it came again.

Slipping out of bed, she shrugged into her robe and tiptoed to investigate.

She almost screamed when she got close enough to see the figure of a man on her balcony. But before the sound left her mouth, moonlight spilled over his face to reveal the Duke of Cornwall.

He'd come for her after all.

But why at midnight?

The balcony was purely decorative; Alice's window didn't even extend to the floor, so when she opened it, she could only lean over the ledge to breathe in Alan's scent.

Tonight, he smelled more of brandy than peppermint.

"Alice, a sight for sore eyes."

She'd wished with all her might to see him again, but now that he'd returned, her blood surged with anger rather than desire. When he lurched forward, as if to kiss her, Alice leaned back. "What are you doing at my window?"

"Don't be angry with me. Not you, my own dear Alice."

She would not be cowed by his sweet words. Not until she had some answers. "Why did you leave me? You put me in a state of disgrace, and now I'm to marry Lord Windemere."

Alan's eyes gleamed back in the moonlight. "I'm sorry. I know it is a terrible fate. I'd have offered for you, of course I would have, you know that. Only I can't."

So he'd heard about her betrothal. Alice was glad to know that, at least, he was listening to news about her. "Why not?"

"I told you. There are things about my life you couldn't understand." Grabbing her hands from across the window ledge, Alan clasped them to his heart. "I wish I could make it different. You are the only one who can make my heart stop aching."

Despite herself, tears welled in Alice's eyes. The only salve to her agony was to know he was in just as much pain. "I can't sleep, for thinking of you."

"You are the echo of my own heartbeat." Alan leaned closer still, resting his forehead against hers.

How could he say such things, and still not marry her? "What is it that stands between us?" Alice whispered. "Why can't you tell me?"

Alan breathed, in and out, the acid on his exhale

prickling Alice's nose. "Osborne must have his way. I'll say no more."

She may as well have been pricked with a knife. So Lord Windemere *did* have something to do with Alan's strange behavior. She should have known. It was too coincidental that Lord Windemere had been among the party that discovered her. Somehow, he'd planned it from the beginning.

"Alice, my heart." Alan pressed forward, his lips descending to hers for a kiss.

But Alice had learned her lesson. She jerked her face out of reach. "You cannot behave so if you don't intend to marry me."

Alan's grip on her hands tightened. "What is there to protect?"

My heart, Alice thought, but she didn't dare say it. "I am not a loose woman. I thought you intended to offer for me last night. Unless you speak with my father, I cannot kiss you again."

Now his grip was a vise, squeezing her bones against each other as he pulled her close. "You will be married soon. You won't need your father's permission to take a lover."

Many married women took lovers. Alice knew that; it was fuel for much of the *ton* gossip. But she doubted many of them plotted their affairs before even reaching the altar.

She stared at Alan. She couldn't read his expression

in the dark. She couldn't see any love in his eyes.

Alice straightened as much as she could in Alan's grip. "Then wait for me. When I am ready for a lover, you will be the first I write."

"Wait for you? Are you really not going to let me in?"

If she let him in…oh, at least she wouldn't be tossing and turning wondering why she was not enough for him. But Alice knew it would only lead to more trouble. To worse heartache.

Still, she couldn't quite summon the words, to turn away the man she loved.

She could only shake her head no.

Alan threw her hands away, nearly tossing her to the ground with his intensity.

"Speak to my father," Alice begged. "There's still time to call off the engagement. I can still marry you."

But Alan had already swung a leg off the balcony onto the awaiting oak tree. He looked back at her one last time.

"I'm still yours," Alice cried.

Alan disappeared into the night.

Chapter Sixteen

The wedding announcement made it into the Saturday paper, so that by the time the *ton* descended upon St. George's Hanover Square for Sunday service, everyone had heard that Alice was to be the next Countess of Windemere.

Since it was her first public appearance since the engagement, Alice's mother took special interest in her outfit. Alice was in her best silk bonnet, a periwinkle blue that matched her linen dress, whose neckline was embroidered with imported Belgian lace.

She was the picture of a perfect fiancée.

She was beset by well-wishers on the steps into service; nestled between her parents in the family pew, Alice could hear people whispering about her.

It's a fair match.

A little early in the Season, considering how many suitors she had about her.

Wasn't the Duke of Cornwall sweet on her?

If only the *ton* could know how she spent every waking moment thinking of the Duke of Cornwall on her balcony.

It had been four days, and still, he had not spoken to her father. Nor had he visited her again, or sent flowers, or sent a message.

Alice couldn't quite regret standing her ground, but she wished they had parted with some more formal understanding. Something more concrete than the hope that they may reunite as lovers one day.

Her best plan was to run into him at church.

Alas, the duke was nowhere to be seen. He wasn't to be found in the second-row Cornwall pew, but he could have chosen to sit with someone else. He could have come late and chosen instead to stand in the back. Alice could just picture him, long and lean and impatient, arms crossed as he leaned against the wooden entrance door. Would he be looking for her, too?

All through the sermon, which had a particular bent on being dutiful, Alice tilted her head this way and that, pretending to examine the arcing ceiling or the sculptures or stained glass, only trying to glimpse the duke out of the corner of her eye.

She was rewarded only with Lisbeth, tucked in three rows back, and a sighting of Lord Windemere. He was ahead of her, alone in a pew. Her heart surprised her by giving a little tug. Someone should have invited him to sit with them. Her family should have invited him to sit with them. Perhaps he had snuck in too late.

Alice shook herself. She wasn't to feel sympathy for the villain Osborne. He sat alone because he was a wretched old miser, whose only hope for getting a wife was to weave a plot to disgrace Alice.

She didn't understand it, yet Alan had all but confirmed: Lord Windemere was the reason Cornwall couldn't offer for her.

Lord Windemere shifted, his head turning ever so slightly, and suddenly his blue eyes connected with hers. It was only for a second – half a second, an instant too short to count, really – but it was as tactile as a burn. Alice shot her gaze to her hands, flushing.

He would think she was thinking of him. Thinking of him the way a fiancée thinks of her future husband. The way a fiancée pictures her husband in privacy, how he'll treat her when doors are closed. How his kiss will sear her. How his hands will touch her.

No, Alice wasn't thinking those things, and she certainly wouldn't let Lord Windemere imagine she was. If she had to marry him – which she still wasn't completely convinced would actually come to pass – it would be a marriage of convenience only. She would submit, as a wife was obliged to do, but her focus would be on her duties as a mistress of Richmond Hall, or as a mother, or as a visiting daughter to Bleneccle Manor. She would never so much as dream of Lord Windemere taking her in both hands and dizzying her with kisses.

The minister cleared his throat mid-sentence, as if he could hear her thoughts. Alice buried deeper into her pew. She didn't dare look up. What if Lord Windemere was still watching? What if the whole church was staring at her, she who thought impure thoughts during a holy hour?

They rose to sing hymns. They sat to pray. They filed down the aisle to receive communion. They sang again. They prayed again. By the time the service finally ended, Alice was convinced she was already in hell, caught in an interminable church service with a wholly inappropriate imagination.

The *ton* took its time filing out of church, taking advantage of proximity to chat with each other. Lisbeth escaped her chaperone aunt to dance over to Alice's pew. "Miss Winpole, many congratulations on your engagement."

Alice flushed again. She had only just been protesting her disinterest in Lord Windemere, and here she was engaged to him. Lisbeth must have thought Alice a shame-faced liar. "Perhaps we can steal away for a few minutes so I can tell you the details of the engagement."

Lisbeth smiled slyly. "I'm sure there are many details I would love to hear. Will you be at the Greville dinner tomorrow night?"

Lady Eastley hadn't consulted Alice on social engagements since the Pemberly ball. With the wedding fast approaching, they would be attending fewer. "I'm not sure. Perhaps my mother and I can call on you today or tomorrow, just in case."

"I await your card." Lisbeth ducked a curtsy. "The Earl of Thorne approaches, so I must take my leave, otherwise be claimed as his next victim."

The earl indeed approached, as did the Marquess

of Asbury, each expressing their many felicitations and great regret they hadn't made their offers soon enough. Alice smiled through it, tried to look the part of a blushing affianced lady. By all counts, she should be thrilled: she had caught herself a husband who had all his teeth, no previous children, and no great mountains of debt.

She was so busy trying to look excited about her upcoming nuptials that she didn't even notice Lord Windemere approaching until he was upon her.

He bowed in that solemn, unsmiling way of his. He and Lady Windemere had called on them two days after the Pemberly ball, a tedious tea during which everyone spoke in masked pleasantness. Her father and Lord Windemere carried the conversation with discussions of their lands; Lord Windemere would be gaining some of the backwaters at the border between Bleneccle Manor and Richmond Hall as part of the marriage settlement. Alice had steadfastly avoided eye contact and conversation as much as politeness allowed.

It was harder to ignore Lord Windemere when he was directly in front of her. Their eyes connected again, and Alice hated it just as much. He looked too kind for what she knew him to be. He would ensnare her as a friend again, only to betray her.

"Lord Windemere will escort you home," her father told Alice. "He'll take you through the park for some fresh air."

Alice looked to Lady Eastley, silently pleading for

her mother to save her. But Lady Eastley simply nodded encouragingly. "Be sure to enjoy the greenery."

They walked as a foursome through the rest of the church crowd. Lord Windemere led her to his waiting brougham. She ignored his offered hand and stepped herself straight into the carriage, then arranged her skirt tightly around her legs so it wouldn't slip close to him. He took the seat opposite her, facing backward as the carriage took off at a slow clop to the park.

Alice folded her hands into her lap and fixed her gaze on the city beyond the window.

"Did you enjoy the sermon?" Lord Windemere asked after a few moments of silence.

She barely remembered what was covered. "It was enlightening."

Her words hung in the air for a little while. "I found it rather dull."

Alice chose not to respond. Let him see what lay ahead for him: the cold shoulder.

"That's a very pretty dress," he said. "It's a good color for you."

"Thank you."

They were nearing the park. Alice estimated another fifteen minutes of this torture and then she would be free.

Except when they got to the park, Lord Windemere knocked on the top of the carriage to bring it to a stop. "We'll take a little walk," he said, directing the driver to meet them at the other end of the Serpentine path.

Alice was of a mind to insist on staying in the carriage. Lord Windemere was malleable enough to heed her. But just when she would have thrown a tantrum, the Marchioness of Leighster passed, walking arm-in-arm with her sisters. The marchioness gave a little wave at the couple, looking smug, as if she were responsible for their engagement.

Which in a way, Alice supposed, was true. Had the marchioness not been among the party that discovered Alice and Alan, the whole thing could have been swept under the rug as a family secret.

Likely Lord Windemere was the one who'd choreographed the marchioness's presence.

Still, it wouldn't do for the marchioness to see Alice throwing a tantrum. So, Alice stepped out of the carriage – again, ignoring her fiancé's offered hand. She followed him on the path, staying a step behind him in the largest protest she could think of against his plans.

"I miss walking in the country," Lord Windemere said. "Do you have a favorite path in Bleneccle Manor?"

Alice had eons of favorite paths at home. She loved walking down to the lake, or up the hill to survey the rolling mountains, or to the Greek folly where she and Margot used to set up tea parties for their dolls. But Lord Windemere didn't deserve to know about them.

"I prefer not to walk," she lied.

Lord Windemere sighed. It wasn't overly dramatic, designed to elicit a response. Rather, his sigh was the first sign that he was tiring of this game.

Alice felt bad, until she remembered she wasn't supposed to feel pity for him.

They encountered Lord and Lady Pemberly, who stopped to chat long enough to wish them felicitations. Ahead were more clumps of people out walking after church. Alice felt exhausted just anticipating the polite chit chat.

She wasn't completely put out, then, when Lord Windemere guided her down a side path, through a little glade of woods that made it semi-private.

"I know you feel done wrong by His Grace the Duke of Cornwall," Lord Windemere said. "I regret that I cannot fill his shoes in your eyes. But I hope you can find the bright side in all of this, eventually. I should hate for you to be so unhappy for the rest of your life."

Alice flinched hearing Alan's styling on Lord Windemere's lips. "Yes, it would be a shame if your devious plan didn't work out after all."

"My devious plan?"

"Do you think it escaped my notice that you are the one who set this all in motion? First, you were the one who told your mother to try to warn me off the duke, saying I would end up in a compromising position if I so much as danced with him. Then you tried to scare me away from him with your claim that he was only dallying with me to toy with you, of all the self-centered stories to spin. And who did you bring with you into the garden but the Marchioness of Leighster?" Alice didn't care that her voice was rising, or that she was surely flushed red, or that she was pointing her finger in Lord Windemere's face in a wholly unladylike fashion. "I don't know how, but I know this was all your doing. Some twisted plan to force me to marry you, since you knew you would never win me the honorable way."

Lord Windemere's face was no longer impenetrable. He stared at her with horror and some other emotion she couldn't interpret, not in her state of rage.

"Your imagination astounds me." His voice trembled, imperious though it was. "But I'm afraid your logic doesn't hold up. My mother and I were trying to prevent this from happening with warnings. We were unfortunately correct in doing so, but not because we wanted it to happen. Indeed, I wouldn't wish your state of disgrace on any woman in my acquaintance."

Alice tried very hard not to let her flinch show.

"The Marchioness of Leighster beseeched me to walk with her when I was about to leave the ball, after you so viciously told me off. I was only following her to see the Pemberly's white lilies. I certainly didn't suspect we would encounter you in such a behavior, though I have to say it didn't surprise me, given how forward you've been with *me* in the past."

Now Alice flamed red. That inexplicable moment in the library had come back to bite her indeed. He was right: she was shameful. Her behavior *was* disgraceful.

"And finally, may I remind you that the one and only person who truly put you in this position is the gentleman who refused to marry you. Last I checked, that was the Duke of Cornwall. Not I."

Alice thought back to Alan's words. *Osborne must have his way.* Alan clearly thought of Lord Windemere as an obstacle, but had Alice misunderstood the implication of malice? Did Alan merely see Lord Windemere as a rival?

Lord Windemere stared at her with disinterest. She reeled forward with her attack out of instinct. "If you didn't plan this, then why on earth would you offer for me?"

He turned away. Alice wondered if this was the moment she lost her saving grace husband.

"Because, my lady, somewhere between our first quadrille and our last, I discovered my ideal countess." Lord Windemere looked back to her. His gaze was, as ever, so intense, so warm. "I'm in love with you."

Chapter Seventeen

Hugh couldn't quite believe the words had left his lips. It was one thing to admit his admiration for Alice to his mother; he certainly hadn't meant to confess his love to his cold, angry fiancée.

But he couldn't let her believe such a wild conspiracy as the one she espoused. He couldn't let her think he'd do anything other than wish for her happiness.

After a sleepless night, Hugh had decided it was worth risking her scorn to treat her the way he wanted to treat her: steal her away for private moments, shower her with presents, send her flowers every day. And he'd selected Sunday as the perfect day to start. His intention had been to renew their friendship with simple conversation, then ease her into his attentions.

Except Alice was determined to be unhappy. The carriage ride had chilled him thoroughly; only sheer perseverance had steered him forward. He'd wanted to find civility. He'd uncovered conspiracy.

And somehow ended up throwing his very heart at her feet.

Now their little glade was silent. Not even a bird chirped, though perhaps that was because his heart beat so loudly in his ears he couldn't hear anything else. Alice stared at him with her wide green eyes. Hugh couldn't have said anything more shocking, and probably nothing less welcome.

He may as well carry through with his plan for the afternoon. Too bad if it made her uncomfortable. He couldn't possibly get more pathetic than what he already claimed to be, a sappy fool in love with a woman who hated him.

Hugh withdrew the jewelry box from his pocket and placed it in her hand. "An engagement gift."

Alice's mouth still hung open in shock as she opened the box. It wasn't anything too flashy – Hugh at least had enough sense not to ask her to wear an oversized gemstone to celebrate a marriage she loathed – just a simple peridot in a gold setting. The pale green stone had sat in one of his grandmother's necklaces. It reminded him of Alice's eyes, so he'd commissioned a new ring for it.

She stared down at the jewelry box. "Thank you," she said dully.

Of course, she hated it. Hugh should have expected nothing less. It was clear she hated everything about the engagement, including him.

He knew it would be best to move on, get the walk behind them. Time would ease everything. He'd get used to her not caring for him, and she'd get used to being his wife.

But he surprised himself with a perverse demand. "Why don't you put it on?"

Alice blinked up at him.

He learned he loved lashing his heart over and over again, for he took the ring from its box, clasped her hand – so small and soft in his palm – and slid the ring onto her gloved finger. It fit loosely. She curled her hand into a fist.

"It matches your eyes," Hugh said. What he would give to know what was racing through her head.

"Thank you," she said again. Then she drew back. A little of the angry suspicion that had laced her words earlier returned to her lips. "Why?"

"Why did I give you a ring?"

"Why do you love me? I was vicious to you. I've been incredibly forward, with you and with the duke. Why would you love me?"

Earlier, when Alice had hurtled her conspiracy at him, there had been no space for anything but her anger. But now, in this helpless question, Hugh sensed an opening.

Which meant his answer mattered.

"There is no reason to love. There is only feeling. And when I'm around you, I feel..." Not quite realizing it, Hugh stepped closer. She was nearly his height. If he reached out, he could touch her. If he inhaled, he would smell her. "I feel happy. You are intelligent; you challenge me to keep learning. You are beautiful; you inspire me to earn your attentions. And you are kind; you make me feel welcome."

The words filled him with yearning for everything he dreamed of for them. Friendship, banter, sweet nothings.

Kisses and keeping each other warm on winter nights. A marriage of partners. A life of conversation.

Alice stared up at him with gleaming peridot irises. Her bosom rose and fell rapidly.

Perhaps that dream was not unattainable after all. "I know your heart belongs to another for now. I don't expect you to say anything back. Only know that I'm marrying you to give you the life you deserve. Not as a favor to your family. Not because I can't get a wife any other way. Because I love you, and I want to see you happy."

And then quite suddenly, Alice – lovely, forward, shameful Alice – surged forward. He inhaled the scent of violets and hair powder as their lips met.

It wasn't chaste, not even to begin. Her lips were soft and tender, and he wanted to explore them for hours. He nearly moaned when she palmed his neck, tugging him tighter. His hands landed on her waist, heating to his very core. Only his barest grip on reality – they were still in that glade, could still be caught by anyone walking by – kept him from tearing off her Belgian lace.

Alice was the one to end the kiss as well, one hand on his shoulder pushing firmly away. Hugh held onto her waist for a little longer. He rested his forehead on hers. "Thank goodness for your forwardness. I was never going to muster up the courage to do that, much as I wanted to."

He couldn't help himself from grinning at her. What a spectacular kiss it had been; how could one *not* be beaming?

But Alice stepped away. That cold expression from the carriage ride returned. "I wanted to know what it would be like. But my heart still belongs to the duke."

Hugh's hands fell uselessly by his side. Of course, he'd expected too much from one kiss. Not five minutes ago, she'd believed Hugh to be the reason for her unhappiness. Hugh would have to remember patience on this journey into her good graces.

"As far as I'm concerned, this will be a marriage of convenience," Alice continued. "I will be dutiful in public, and I will give you an heir. But I'm not interested in love or friendship with you."

Her words did their job. He stepped back, withdrew even his gaze from her. "Then I beg your pardon. Let me escort you home so you may be free of me for the day."

Patience, he reminded himself. Even if his heart broke a hundred times along the way.

Chapter Eighteen

Two days later, Alice still didn't know what had come over her.

She could barely sleep for reliving that dreadful walk with Hugh. For one, why had she thought it a good idea to provoke him with an accusation? If he were the sort of devil to plot against her, he certainly wasn't going to admit it.

Which was why she had pressed on after he claimed to love her. A convenient excuse, if ever she heard one. Only Hugh's answer had been so dear. So specific. So much more wildly attuned to her than Alan's poetic lines about moonlight and pretty names.

But why, oh why, had she then been possessed to kiss him?

She was supposed to hate Hugh. She was supposed to ignore the way his eyes widened so nicely, his lips lifting in the hope of smile. He was tricking her, she *knew* it.

But Alice hadn't been thinking with any type of rationality. She'd been brimming with his words, and all in a moment had wanted to know what it was like to kiss this boyish man who was to be her husband.

What she was absolutely never going to admit to anyone – especially not herself – was how much she enjoyed the kiss. It was different from the thrilling danger of Alan claiming her in the darkness. Hugh's kiss had lit her whole body with a dream. She floated on clouds. Time, space, thoughts…these were all abstracts. The only truth in the moment of that kiss had been tactile: his lips on hers, his hands holding her firm, his hair curling against her palm.

Though it was nothing compared to the passion she felt for Alan, in the moment after that kiss, when she was returning to her senses and before she remembered her hatred for Hugh, Alice had loved that great, innocent grin that swept across his face.

And *that* was why she'd had to serve the great coup de grace, to make it clear to Hugh and herself both that she was never going to forgive him.

Still, Alice didn't know what had come over her. Or why it hurt so much to see that solemn mask erase Hugh's smile as she proclaimed his friendship was not of interest.

She was grateful for the distraction that afternoon: Margot replaced Lady Eastley as chaperone and stole Alice away for a shopping trip to New Bond Street.

"You're looking glum for a bride-to-be," Margot said as soon as the carriage pulled off from the Winpole house.

"Am I?" Alice tried to sit up straighter, as if that would fix the problem.

"Mama told me about what happened with the Duke of Cornwall at the Pemberly ball, though I do think she left out some sordid details. She and Papa are quite shocked at your behavior, but I remember how you used to have our dolls run off with parsons and stable boys. I'm only impressed you set your sights so high."

How Alice had missed Margot. Even as she teased, she came to sit next to Alice and wrapped a sisterly arm around her shoulders.

"Now tell me what's going through that head of yours. Are you in love with His Grace?"

Alice wished it were so simple. "Yes, I think so. It seems all I do is think about him and how I got into this mess."

"I don't understand it either. Why would he flout the rules of good society so openly? Did he promise you marriage on your walk?"

Alice blushed. In retrospect, she had put up no challenge to Alan. A couple of compliments, a dark corner, and she very nearly gave up her entire innocence. But she had to remember that the whole family thought he was about to offer for her.

"He never even hinted at it. I only assumed."

"We all assumed." Margot waved her wrist, as if a flick of the hand could wipe the whole sordid matter into history. "Now, let's put aside His Disgracefulness for a moment, even though you love him. You're marrying Lord Windemere. How do you feel about that?"

Trust Margot to cut to the heart of the matter. Yet Alice couldn't very well tell her sister that she suspected Lord Windemere was the one standing between herself and marriage to Alan. For one, she didn't understand the scheme herself. For another, admitting Alan had visited her at night to implicate Lord Windemere would only lead to more trouble.

Margot took Alice's silence in hand. "I've always quite liked Hugh myself, though he is an odd duck. You had to feel sorry for him, didn't you, with every year someone else in his family dying. But he didn't mope. He looked after his mother, and he read his books, and he tinkered, and if he opened his mouth, it was to pay us a compliment."

"Don't you think he's rather..." Alice thought of his admission: *I'd never have found the courage to do that.* "Wishy washy? He only does what his mother tells him."

Margot tilted her head in consideration. "I suppose you would too, if Lady Windemere were your mother."

"And he still tinkers, you know. I heard he has a whole workshop. He uses the tools himself. Isn't that unseemly?"

"Yes, I suppose it is. But to play the devil's advocate —" Margot held a gloved hand in the air to pause Alice's objections. "— better that unseemly habit than gambling and ladies of easy virtue, don't you think?"

Alice settled back in her chair. "Are those the only two choices? Are gentlemen either perversely working with their hands or simply perverse?"

"I don't know about most gentlemen, but the Duke of Cornwall has a reputation of the latter." Margot squeezed Alice tight. "I know your heart aches for him, but honestly, Al, the more I hear of His Disgracefulness, the more I'm glad he didn't offer for you. He's a rake, through and through."

Alice conjured Alan's face. She remembered it more dimly than in the first few days after the Pemberly ball; now she mostly thought of lost eyes behind a charmingly broken nose.

She wished he would find another way to visit her again.

"Rakes can be reformed," she whispered.

The carriage pulled to a stop in front of the haberdasher. Margot gave her one last squeeze, then swept into the public sphere. Their task that day was to order Alice's hats for her trousseau, and Margot determined they would do it with good cheer.

It was amusing to watch Margot in London, when Alice had only ever known her sister as an unmarried country lady. At home, Margot had resisted good dresses, gossiped with the servants, and preferred to gallop on her horse than help Lady Eastley with the week's menu. But now that she was Countess of Wickham, Margot presented the very picture of a *ton* lady.

She greeted fellow shoppers with the appropriate mix of enthusiasm and distance. She commanded the shop helpers. She knew just enough gossip to get a conversation going without descending into unseemliness, and she charmed the gentlemen accompanying ladies with ever-so-subtle flirtation.

The only hint of her old mischief was when she donned a sample gentleman's hat and wore it for the entirety of their visit.

"Is that the new style, Lady Wickham?" a familiar voice smiled as Alice tested a pale blue ribbon against her complexion. Seeing in the mirror that the voice belonged to Lisbeth, Alice let out a cry of delight and forgot all about the task at hand.

"If the three of us started the trend, I daresay it would become the new fashion," Margot rejoined.

"What brings you out for a new bonnet?" Alice asked.

"Not as exciting a reason as yours, for sure. Mama's best hat got soaked in the rain last month, so she wants a new one before the Ascot race next week." Lisbeth gestured to her mother, who chatted with the shopkeeper at the counter. Then she set her wicked smirk on Alice. "How does it feel to be shopping for one's trousseau? Are you overcome with excitement?"

Alice wished they were alone, so she could fill Lisbeth in on all the twists and turns that had led to her engagement. Instead, she aimed for an appropriate level of enthusiasm. "I suppose it will be more exciting when I'm actually married, rather than just anticipating everything."

Margot, playing with ribbons herself now, waved the idea away. "Enjoy the anticipation while you can. Nothing ever lives up to the hype."

"What does fill one's time after one marries?" Lisbeth

asked, following Margot's lead and testing a gentleman's rounded hat on her head. It was quite the look, given her short stature and decidedly womanish curves. "Is it really just menu planning and house decorating?"

"So far, it seems to be an endless list of problems to solve," Margot said. "The ceiling in such-and-such room is leaking. The esteemed personage in town is offended by the other esteemed personage, and what are we to do about it? There's a fever sweeping through town, and couldn't I visit the sick room? That sort of thing."

Alice returned to her ribbons. She'd been so focused on getting to the Season, and then enjoying it, that she'd never really thought about what came next. Windemere was a large estate, with several hundred tenants. Was she up to the task to be its countess?

"I suppose that's better than the alternative," Lisbeth sighed, adding a pink bow to the brim of her top hat.

Alice's interest piqued. "What alternative?"

"Retiring as an old spinster to some family cottage. For me, it would be the stone hut at the back of our park, with a view of the river. I'd spend my days knitting for the village and sneaking sweets to my brother's children."

That didn't necessarily sound worse than marrying the wrong man.

"Miss Dawes, that is far too specific not to be a fantasy," Margot said. "Pray tell, why do you think you'll end up in a cottage rather than whisked away? I heard Lord Gresham was quite taken with you after your quadrille at the Walthorpe ball. He'd be quite a catch."

Evidently, Alice had been far too absorbed in her own drama for the past week, for now she was discovering all new facets to Lisbeth she hadn't dreamed. Lord Gresham was young, handsome, and in line to become a Marquess.

Lisbeth didn't exactly blush, but her eyes did glimmer with a secret satisfaction. "Lord Gresham danced with nearly every eligible lady. I'm sure he's already forgotten me. Besides, I haven't gotten myself a marriage offer as quickly as our Miss Winpole."

Alice tried to smile, but it came out as a grimace. Lisbeth was too smart not to notice.

"You are happy about it, aren't you, Alice? Or were you holding out for an offer from the Duke of Cornwall?"

If only it were as simple as that. Alice looked to Margot, as if her older sister could answer for her complicated heart.

Margot set down her hat. "I've got a brilliant idea. Why don't we go down the street and get some ices? That way we won't starve while Alice catches you up on her paramours."

They were just turning down New Bond Street to the ice parlor, after securing Lady Ipswich's permission, when who should step out from the boot store but the Duke of Cornwall himself.

Alice hadn't seen him since he disappeared off her balcony. When she'd begged him to speak to her father.

He looked well. His face was even more striking than

her memory conjured, fit for a Greek sculpture. Alice's heart skipped faster, anticipating the delight of having his dark eyes on her. This was her chance to set things right. To say all the things she'd been saving up. She only wanted him to kiss her every day for the rest of her life.

Margot and Lisbeth clamped down on Alice's arms on either side. Alan turned their direction. His eyes dotted down to them. Alice tried to catch his gaze, to hold it with her own, to feel that connection. *My Alice.*

The ladies dipped into curtsies.

"Your Grace," Margot said, a slight edge lining her tone that Alice hoped only she could hear.

He contemplated them for one half moment more. Good manners alone would earn Alice a greeting. She would hear him say her name in that deep, delicious voice of his.

But Alan did not comply. In the instant when he should have responded to Margot, he simply walked away. He passed them in two lazy steps. Alice smelled his mystifying cologne. She could have reached out and touched him. She could have thrown herself in his arms.

She stood still and silent.

"Well, I never..." Margot stared after the duke in disbelief. "The cut direct? From *that* scoundrel?"

Lisbeth held tight to Alice's hand. "I see there's quite a story for me to hear."

Alice blinked back hot, stinging tears. "Perhaps he didn't see us."

"Oh, Alice. Come, let's get that ice before everyone stares." Margot had to tug Alice to remind her to move. The whole walk there, Margot tutted under breath about the nerve of the duke, while Lisbeth simply clung to Alice's arm.

Alice didn't process words. Her heart was burning, too deep inside for her to douse. She'd been wrong, all wrong. Lord Windemere wasn't the reason Alan hadn't offered. *She* was. He didn't want to marry her. He didn't want to acknowledge her.

The Duke of Cornwall only wanted to use her as a mistress.

And she'd almost let him.

Chapter Nineteen

Hugh collected Alice after church again for another go at winning her over. He'd ignored her for the most part that week, except for a delivery of fresh-cut myrtle on Wednesday morning, which was more for show to Lord and Lady Winpole than in hopes of putting a smile on her face. In fact, he imagined she turned red with fury at the sight of them. *I am not interested in love or friendship with you.*

So, he braced himself for another frigid carriage ride following weekly services. His first sign of a change was that she took his offered hand to step into his coach. Then, once the horses started off, Alice was the one to initiate conversation. "Are we to walk in Hyde Park again?"

Hugh shook his head. He couldn't imagine ever venturing onto the Serpentine again, not with such an ugly scene from the previous week imprinted like a tattoo on his heart. "I thought perhaps you would like to visit our London home, to see where you will be living."

She didn't exactly smile. But neither did she sneer at the idea. She was wearing a pale green that day, with the same scooped neckline as the week before, which invited one to admire her shapely chest and hinted at that waist Hugh knew to be soft and supple. He tried not to let his thoughts dip into indecency, but he throbbed anyway in memory of her kiss.

As far as I am concerned, this is a marriage of convenience.

Hugh noted the peridot ring sparkling on her right hand. It made her fingers look slender and delicate. Perfect for a husband to hold.

He forced himself to look out the window. He had vowed not to try too hard at conversation that afternoon. No need to discuss the gray weather if she didn't want to. Hugh was fine with silent companionship, as long as she wasn't stewing in her corner thinking dreadful thoughts about him.

"How is Lady Windemere's health?" Alice asked.

"Her spirits are high, though she is physically weak." Just that morning, his mother had decided to try to come with him to church, only to be overcome with a coughing attack at the top of the stairs.

"Is she improving?" Between the lines, he understood Alice was asking for the diagnosis.

Lady Windemere had instructed Hugh not to share the doctors' grim predictions that she would not live past the end of summer. She did not want maudlin visits from curious friends, and moreover, she did not want the pity. Hugh had generally tried his best not to give specifics.

But Alice was about to be family. In fact, as the new Countess of Windemere, she might bear the burden of the last few months of Lady Windemere's care. Hugh decided he owed her a modicum of honesty. "She is in decline. The doctors predict she only has a few months left."

Pity flooded Alice's expression. Hugh looked away. He didn't want to receive it any more than his mother did.

"I'm sorry. How terrible, to know you have precious little time left with your mother."

The diagnosis had come in January, just before the Season started. Lady Windemere had received it with her usual unemotional quiet, save for the command that Hugh was to use the Season to find a countess. Hugh had, for the most part, modeled his reaction after his mother's. It was only in the dark of the night that he allowed himself to contemplate what he would do without his mother – his only living loved one.

"It does not do to dwell on such things," Hugh responded to Alice, a phrase his mother had said a hundred times as he grew up in their strange little world of grief.

Presently, they arrived to the Windemere town house. It wasn't particularly different than any other London home in their set, but Hugh took his time giving Alice the tour. His butler, Alby, and housekeeper, Mrs. Nash, joined them, filling in various details about upkeep that Alice might want to know. The crystal chandelier in the dining room, for example, took three days to clean, so her ladyship would want to give them plenty of notice before any significant dinners. As for the ballroom, Mrs. Nash feared it needed a new job of parquet before any dance could be given, since the current wood was buckling or missing in several places.

"It's been a generation or so since we have done our duties as hosts," Hugh explained by way of apology.

They'd finished with the public rooms, and Hugh instructed Mrs. Nash to bring tea service to the drawing room. He waited for the servants to leave them alone to peek again at Alice, to see if she had regained any color after hearing of all the work that awaited her as mistress of the town house.

"It could use some improvements," he admitted. "I have put it off, supposing my mother or a new countess might have an opinion. If it is interesting to you, I am happy to leave the project entirely in your hands."

Alice was still staring around with wide eyes. Hugh feared he'd overwhelmed her. Or perhaps he had guessed wrong; perhaps the task of putting a house to rights was the furthest thing from interesting to Alice.

But then Alice settled her focus on him, offering a small nod. "It has beautiful bones. I shall look forward to the challenge of putting it to rights."

Hugh let out a breath of relief. She may not accept his friendship, and she certainly didn't accept his love, but at least she would have something to start off, to make her happy.

"However, I think you skipped a room in the tour, my lord. Where is your workshop?"

Hugh froze. He didn't think anyone knew about his workshop, at least not the one in London. So, he parlayed. "I think you may call me Hugh at this point."

Alice opened her mouth to respond, then shut it again. Finally, she settled on, "Thank you. May I see your workshop, Hugh?"

His heart skipped. His Christian name on her lips was almost as sweet as another kiss. "May I call you Alice?"

Her lips twitched into the smallest of smiles at his bargain. "I suppose it is only fair."

"In that case, Alice—" A more beautiful name had never been invented. Hugh offered her his arm. "—allow me to escort you downstairs."

The workshop was entered via a door beneath the staircase, just narrow enough for one person to pass through. Hugh went first, so he could light the candles as they went. "I must warn you, it is a bit dim and dusty down here. It's not quite fit for a lady."

In fact, with every step, Hugh regretted agreeing to show it to her. Alice's dress was bound to get dirty, and she would surely feel uncomfortable in the cold, dark cave. Worse, she would see exactly how he shamed the title of earldom with his oiled tools and rough drawings.

Alice kept her silence as she circled the room. Her gaze raked over the earthen walls and rough-hewn work-table. She paused in front of the glass chest of tools, as if to puzzle over what each one was for, and again at the drafting table. When she caressed his sketch for a dual-rotating gear, Hugh shivered, as if her fingers were brushing his cheek instead of his lines.

Presently, she turned her attention to the hulking mechanical scythe that was so close to completion on his table. She darted her bright green gaze to him. "What is it that you're building?"

The candlelight flickered across her face so that Hugh couldn't quite tell her expression. Was it a frown of distaste? Polite curiosity? Or did she truly want to learn about it?

"If it works, it will be a mechanic scythe for hay. So that instead of twenty men to clear an acre, it will only take two."

Alice leaned over the table. Her purpose was to get a better view of the various parts of the scythe, but the pose offered Hugh a delectable candlelit view of her neckline. He yanked his eyes to the tool chest. He would not, under any circumstances, let his thoughts linger *there*.

"Wherever did you get the idea for such a thing?" Alice asked. There was a little more animation behind her words now. If Hugh dared hope such a thing – which he didn't – he'd think she might be interested. Perhaps even impressed.

"I suppose it was when I returned home most recently. Our wealth relies on the land, but truly it depends on a workforce of men willing to break their backs for us. If we can invent new tools to make their tasks easier, then perhaps we can all turn our industry toward finding more wealth. Particularly for the common man."

Alice's gaze had shifted from the scythe to sit squarely on him. Hugh didn't want to miss a second of her attention, but the green glimmer was too intense when they two were alone in the dark, cool cellar. He looked past her to the wall.

"How did you come to care for the common man?" Alice asked.

He cleared his throat. "I'm not sure my motivations are so pure. There is growing unrest in the lower classes, and I'm mainly interested in finding a solution that does not involve a guillotine."

"Is there? I thought the only troubles were with our foreign enemies."

It didn't surprise him; a well-bred lady did not need to worry over such things like banks running out of coin or ever-rising bread taxes. "Indeed. I'm afraid it is on all fronts. In the north, the coal miners are rumbling about their work conditions. In Nottingham, the Luddites sneak into weaving factories and break the knitting frames. If you'd like to learn more, I can collect some news clippings for you." Hugh paused as his words settled in the air, realizing a little too late he may have frightened her.

"Yes, thank you." Alice stepped back from the worktable. "I'd hate to remain so woefully ill-informed."

Hugh didn't quite know how to respond to that. He supposed they had better return to the drawing room. His mother was hoping to make it down to join them, and certainly enough time had passed for the maids to help her down the staircase.

But just as he was about to shepherd Alice back up, she spoke again. "Lord Windemere – Hugh – I'm afraid I owe you an apology. For, well, everything last week."

Hugh didn't dare breathe.

"I said awful things to you. I understand now, it wasn't your doing. Everything that happened. It wasn't well done of me. I sincerely apologize. And I hope that we can have a friendship, despite my behavior."

Despite the dim light, Hugh could see the tears brimming in her green eyes. He closed the distance between them in a few fell steps. "Apology accepted. We need never mention it again."

She exhaled, an uneven sigh that tugged straight at Hugh's heart. How he wished he could kiss her, or even take her two hands in his. He settled for holding his hand out for a gentleman's handshake.

"To friendship."

Alice looked at his palm in suspicion. Then she twitched her lips into a small, flirtatious smile. "Don't you think, given the circumstances, it would be better sealed with a kiss?"

Somehow, Hugh didn't lose all his senses. He even managed to tease her. "Miss Winpole, you are a vixen."

She grinned, a cat who ate the canary, and tipped her head forward, eyes closed, awaiting her kiss.

Two could play that game. Removing his glove, Hugh dared run his thumb along the cut of her jaw. She gasped, a tiny little sound that shot straight to his groin. Her skin was soft and smooth and hot on his bare skin. Hugh wanted to devour her. Instead, he drew the moment longer, bringing his mouth not to her lips but to her neck, hovering over her skin. He inhaled: she smelled of powder and incense and woman. He exhaled: she whimpered.

Losing his control, he closed his mouth on hers, drinking in the sweet taste of Alice. She met him eagerly, anchoring her arms around his neck and pressing tight and close. Her words from the week before thundered across his heart – *I am not interested in your love* – but Hugh dismissed them. However long this moment lasted, he would lose himself in it. And always remember it.

His hands were just about to wander to inappropriate places when Alby politely cleared his throat. "Lady Windemere awaits you in the drawing room, my lord."

"Thank you, Alby." Hugh didn't release Alice until Alby had retreated back up the stairs. Even in the candlelight, he could see the flush that had spread across her neck and chest. He waited, bracing for her to repent her words. She had kissed him last week, too, and lanced him in payment.

But today, a sweet, embarrassed smile played across her face. "I'm afraid I've been terribly forward again."

"It's not so forward when we're engaged to be married." Hugh pressed the pad of his thumb to her lips. He'd never been so wicked. She would be the death of him, that was still for sure, but at least he'd enjoy it on his way down. "Shall we?"

Chapter Twenty

Alice's whole body thrummed as she climbed the stairs ahead of Hugh. She put extra emphasis on each step to make her muslin skirt swing, since he was just behind her, no doubt watching her every move. So strange. This time last week, she'd been fuming at him, and now she floated.

Alby awaited them at the top of the stairs with just a hint of amusement behind his otherwise professionally impassive expression. Alice waited for Hugh to offer an arm to lead her back to the drawing room. The house truly was magnificent, all the more because it was about to be hers. Alice looked again at the wallpaper, which glimmered with gold-leaf trimmings, and the Romanesque carvings across the ceiling. One of Hugh's predecessors had dreamed of glory and shown it off in these beautiful little accents.

It was hardly anything less than she would have expected of a duke's residence.

Alice banished the thought as soon as it danced through her head, the same as she'd done in that moment when Hugh leaned in for a kiss and she'd thought, *Not quite as nice as Alan's.* Well, Hugh had taught her a lesson, hadn't he, feinting a kiss to torment her, only to make her realize how desperately she wanted her future husband to ravish her.

Alice had spent the past week studiously erasing all thoughts of Alan whenever they crossed her mind. She didn't understand him, why he would cut her direct after visiting her at night, but she knew now he had no good intentions towards her. For whatever reason, she rose no higher than a lump of coal in his esteem, and there was no changing it. So, she resolved to change her own attitude.

It had been easier than she'd expected. Once she decided not to think of the Duke of Cornwall, she remembered what a strangely vivid connection she and Hugh had. He was intelligent, considerate, and surprisingly funny in their more off-the-cuff conversations. And he was handsome. As she fell asleep each night, Alice conjured his face: that piercing expression behind his spectacles, his hair overflowing around his temple in rain-drenched curls, his lips curving hopefully. Alice clung to that moment in the library, before all the ugliness, when she had so desperately needed to touch him. Claim him.

Now she had even more fodder for her nightly recounting. In candlelight, Hugh resembled an angel in a Dutch master painting. He fiddled nervously with his pockets as he watched her invade his private, manly space. Passion brimmed behind his words as he explained his scythe. And he was willing to forgive her, despite her awfulness. Because he loved her.

No, Hugh was not at all a bad fiancée to have ended up with.

Lady Windemere awaited them in the drawing room. When Hugh had shown it to Alice – just a quarter hour previously – the curtains were tied open, letting daylight filter in. Now the drapery was drawn, darkening the place as a sickroom, with candles lit as if it were the middle of the night. Lady Windemere lay across the chaise lounge, two pillows behind her and a blanket wrapped around her skirts.

Alice had understood Lady Windemere was sick, but now her stomach somersaulted. Hugh would be devastated to lose his mother.

Hugh dropped his arm, no doubt to go tend to his mother, but Lady Windemere greeted them from where she sat.

"The servants informed me I have been waiting all this time because you were in the basement. Unchaperoned. You do like to run off into dark corners alone with men, don't you, Miss Winpole?"

Alice's whole body flushed, though surely no one could see it in the candlelight. She waited a moment, giving Hugh a chance to admonish his mother on her behalf. He didn't.

"Lord Windemere was kind enough to show me his workshop," Alice said finally. No need to acquiesce that they had, indeed, gotten up to no good while down there.

"A workshop is no place for a lady. Do sit. My neck aches craning up to look at the two of you standing."

Alice perched on the settee. Hugh chose the chair

next to his mother instead. Alice tried not to read anything into it. She'd been having such a wonderful day so far. She mustn't let Lady Windemere ruin it, for surely Lady Windemere didn't mean to. Hugh's mother was old and sickly; she was likely in pain, perhaps even scared to reckon with death.

"Well, you're to be the lady of the house. Go ahead and serve the tea." Lady Windemere beckoned to the tea service, which Alice hadn't even noticed in the dark corner next to the settee.

"I take mine black," Lady Windemere continued, "and Lord Windemere's will be three-quarters tea, one-quarter milk, with three lumps of sugar."

The directive alone made Alice want to faint from too much sugar. She looked to Hugh for confirmation. He gave a nod that could only be described as wishy-washy.

The thrumming from their kiss officially disappeared. Where was the man who was so confident a mechanical scythe would solve a class war?

Alice decided to go on the offensive with some good old-fashioned small talk. "I'm so sorry you're weren't feeling up to the service today, Lady Windemere. It was a good sermon on kindness to others."

Lady Windemere took a ferocious sip of tea. Hugh only set his cup aside.

"Tell me, Miss Winpole, do you attend services for the sermons or for the gossip?"

Alice's teacup rattled against the saucer as she clung

to her dignity. This was not small talk. Nor was it even polite.

"Mother, perhaps you'd rather be resting," Hugh said.

Lady Windemere waved her hand dismissively in his direction. "I haven't had my chance to interview your future wife. She is to be the new Lady Windemere. I should like the chance to get to know her."

As if they didn't know each other already. As if the distance between Bleneccle Manor and Richmond Hall was leagues instead of miles.

"They are big shoes to fill indeed, Lady Windemere." Alice didn't think she quite said it convincingly, seeing as she had to force the words through clenched teeth.

"I hope you are not under the impression we shall pretend I don't know the circumstances around your engagement."

Alice looked to Hugh, as if he would put a stop to his mother. As if he had the guts to remind his mother to be polite.

He was grimacing, to be sure, but he wasn't objecting.

"I'm sure you can understand how embarrassed I am about it, Lady Windemere." Alice hated how her voice shook as she tried so hard to sound mature.

"Good. You should be."

"Lord Windemere is kind enough to look past it, and we have agreed it doesn't need to be discussed." Alice pierced him with a look that said, *You should be speaking up to her, not me.* She rather feared he couldn't see it though, what with the darkness and Hugh barely looking her way. "I wonder if you could find it in your heart to do similarly."

"They say to forgive and forget." Lady Windemere paused, hacking a little into her handkerchief. Alice held her own breath, hoping that her next words were just as promising. "However, I'm not one to listen to what others say. You have come by this engagement in a dishonorable manner, Miss Winpole. I would advise you to mind your every move until you have proven yourself honorable."

Alice took a breath in. Pushed that breath out. *The lady is dying*, she reminded herself. *She'd be this awful no matter what*, which was generally agreed to be true among the Richmond Hall neighbors.

But still, even after that pause, Alice stewed. What an unnecessary, horrible thing to say to the woman who would soon be in charge of your household.

In the silence of the room, a clock ticked loudly. Alice sewed her lips into a silent line. If Lady Windemere had nothing kind to say, Alice need not say anything either. There were only twelve minutes left until an honorable lady could excuse herself.

Twelve minutes of silence.

Alice fixed her gaze on the family portrait that hung above the fireplace: young Hugh solemnly standing between his two parents. Even in the artwork, Lady Windemere scowled at her. When it was Alice's house, she would remove all pictures of the dowager countess from sight.

Hugh cleared his throat. He started to mutter something about the weather, but Lady Windemere cut him off.

"I am tired. Call Alby to take me upstairs. You had better take Miss Winpole home."

Alice knew she should be insulted, but all she felt was victory. Rising, she pulled the velvet rope to ring for the butler.

"You can't remain another ten minutes?" Hugh asked his mother.

His mother only glared at him.

Hugh looked from his mother to Alice and back again. Finally, he stood. He offered Alice a stiff arm and led her to the foyer, instructing Alby to call for the coach. They waited in silence. Alice was too angry to trust herself with words, and besides, didn't want the servants to overhear.

In the carriage, however, Hugh was the first to speak. "Are you incapable of finding polite conversation topics?"

Alice stared at him, trying to read behind his opaque eyes to see if there was something more to his words. "Are you quite serious? Were you in that room?"

He crossed his arms, which Alice took as an admission that he knew very well his mother's behavior was out of line. "My mother is a severe woman. You know that. I would expect as my future wife, you would want to brook a good relationship with her."

"I do. How am I to get in her good graces, though, when every word she has for me is an insult? And when my fiancé won't stand up for me? Or do you agree that I should be watching my every step?"

Hugh glared right back at her. "This is not some public spectacle where your honor is being disparaged. Then I would stand up for you, of course. My mother, however, is simply trying to straighten out a relationship with you."

Alice couldn't believe her ears. She couldn't believe her anger, either. She was close to shouting. "If she wanted a relationship with me, she should start from a place of forgiveness, not a place of judgment."

The carriage rattled to a stop in front of the Winpole house. Alice threw Hugh one last glare. "And pardon me for expecting my fiancé to stand by my side whether we're in public or private."

"I believe we've already established you don't get a choice of fiancé. This is your only option." He vaulted out of the carriage, to hand her out and accompany her up the stairs. The door opened, and Hugh cut Alice an angry bow. "You may take it or leave it. Good day, Miss Winpole."

Her heart thumped as he slammed his carriage door.

Chapter Twenty-One

Hugh would have forgotten all about the horse race had Alby not interrupted him twenty minutes before he was due to leave. "Sir, you will be late to retrieve Miss Winpole."

There was a tone to Alby's voice that Hugh knew from childhood, the tone that warned him to run up to the playroom before his father got home or he had crumbles of stolen biscuits on his shirt. It didn't quite belong in Alby's voice now that Hugh was lord and master, but Hugh would no more tell him off than he'd ask his mother to change his tea.

It did, however, irritate Hugh. He'd indulged himself in an overnight plunge into his workshop, taking apart the scythe and reassembling it again to see if he could fix the problem of the rear gear not fully engaging. After a quick rest from dawn until noon, he'd descended again, looking forward to another afternoon of problems limited to the mechanical world.

Yet here was Alby, a physical reminder that in fact, Hugh could not ignore Miss Winpole or the mess that was Hugh's engagement. Or rather, that if he was going to ignore it, Hugh's servants would not be a part of it.

Hugh had never snapped at anyone the way he snapped at Alice in the carriage. He didn't regret it – no, he refused to regret it – for she truly had been unreasonable. Hugh had little hope he would ever earn Alice's reciprocated love. He'd even accepted that she would treat him with cold anger for the duration of their engagement, if not marriage. But he did not see how she could justify being so rude to his dying mother.

No matter that Lady Windemere had been rude herself – she was the senior lady in the room. That was her prerogative. Beneath Lady Windemere's digs, Hugh could hear his mother trying to banish her doubts about Alice. His fiancée need only have answered honestly, or perhaps even apologized, to earn Lady Windemere's forgiveness.

Instead, Alice had parried, blocked, and turned to stone.

Hugh thumped up from his workshop to change for the horse race. Lady Eastley had arranged for him to escort Alice alone, which bordered on indecent but was overlooked because their marriage was only two weeks away. "I worry you two need more time to acquaint yourselves, given the circumstances," Lady Eastley had explained, in a rushed whisper at church. Hugh read between the lines: *given that Alice hates you.*

Well, and just when he thought they'd moved past all the hate and accusations, Alice had gone and shown she didn't care one whit for Hugh's mother. Which translated to not truly caring one whit about Hugh.

What a fool he was, thinking two wonderful kisses would earn him a slot in her esteem.

And now he was back in the black pit he'd been trying to avoid. Hugh tried to calm his swirling self-pity as his man shaved off the angry stubble collecting on his face. *You already knew she didn't love you. This was a fool's errand from the start.* He smoothed his expression in the mirror. What he would give for his mother's cool veneer; Hugh favored his father instead, whose emotions had always stormed across his face.

He would escort Alice to the races, as promised. He would be the picture of a perfect fiancé. And he wouldn't let her get under his skin.

It was an easy resolution to keep until, of course, Hugh arrived at the Winpole house. Alice wore a dress the color of a budding rose, fashionably of the thinnest cotton. He could see the outline of her underclothes beneath it, which plummeted his thoughts in a dangerous direction. He pinched his own thigh: *She will break your heart, idiot.*

In front of her parents, Alice was all sweet smiles and even blushed when Hugh kissed her hand. But almost as soon as he handed her up to the passenger side of his curricle, Alice frosted into the image of a perfect, silent lady.

"Are you comfortable?" Hugh asked as they pulled into the streets. He'd selected his two-person barouche for the drive, since the whole purpose was to show off their shiny engagement, but it was less comfortable than a closed coach. Alice sat with her spine straight, barely touching the cushioned seatback. The hand not holding her parasol clutched the side of the barouche as they jostled over the Mayfair cobblestones.

"Quite," she responded through clenched teeth.

Hugh turned his focus to the road. He couldn't fathom why *she* would be cool with *him* when she was the one who had behaved so badly. All their troubles could be traced back to *her* bad behavior. So why did she make him feel as if he were in the wrong?

The races were a journey, on the outskirts of town in Ascot. Hugh had to keep his attention not only on the road but also on fellow coaches, as they encountered one peer after another. To the Marchioness of Leighster, both he and Alice beamed generous smiles. Then, of course, Alice returned to ignoring him.

Hugh's simmering anger returned. She could not care for him and behave this way. The apology in the basement, her interest in his workshop, even the kiss — that had all been feigned. Perhaps she'd had good intentions. Likely she was trying to convince herself to be content with the match she had. But her present actions spoke far louder than her words, or even her kiss.

She detested her fate. And she was making him detest it, too.

"Have you insulted any other dying ladies in our time apart?" Hugh heard himself ask.

Alice's mouth widened into an O of surprise before she snapped it back into the mask of boredom. "It was *she* who insulted *me*, if you recall."

"Forgive a mother for wanting to ascertain her future daughter-in-law has any feeling for her son."

"Feeling has no place in marriages," Alice said stiffly. He knew she didn't believe it: he need only remember the starry looks that graced her eyes at all the balls to know Alice wanted romance.

"There is always feeling. The question is how you prioritize it."

"And how will you prioritize me?" Alice turned toward Hugh, her parasol jostling against his hat. "Will I always be second-fiddle to your mother? When she insults me at breakfast and luncheon, will you order me to return at dinner for another round?"

Hugh had to remind himself to hold the reins loosely. They were away from the crush of the city now, on a wider dirt road with fewer carriages. "Lady Windemere is dying, if you recall. She was carried down the stairs to take tea with you. She couldn't even handle a little bit of daylight in the room. And for this effort, you rewarded her by refusing to speak, all because of a few unfortunate words."

"A few unfortunate words? The entire interview was designed to humiliate me." Alice flounced backward. Hugh sensed she would have crossed her arms were they not in London. "Besides, I cannot believe Lady Windemere wants to be treated as an invalid."

"Can you believe that I might want my future wife to

show some tenderness to my mother? No matter what my mother says?"

"That is precisely my point. Your allegiance is to your mother, not me, no matter how she treats me. I won't accept that fate happily."

Hugh stared at this woman who was to be his wife. She was lovely with anger, though he didn't want to acknowledge it. Her eyes shone, her body flushed; her whole being hummed with emotion, so opposite of the frozen picture of decorum that had sat next to him all through Mayfair.

He wanted her, no matter how much she hated him.

No matter how much he hated himself for it.

He turned his attention back to the road. And swore. Somehow, somewhere during the argument, they had turned off the main road. Their current path was barely large enough for the wide axels of the barouche. If he reached out a hand, he would easily touch the linden trees lining the road. Beyond the trees, he saw nothing but more forest.

"What is it?" Alice asked, responding to his curse.

Hugh was absolutely not, under any circumstance, going to admit they were lost. "Nothing."

But Alice was looking about. She was a smart girl – it was, unfortunately, one of the things he loved about her – and surely noticed the lack of carriages ahead or behind them. "Have we gone the wrong way?"

Hugh didn't say anything.

"Why aren't we turning around?" Alice demanded.

"Because I'm the driver and I haven't decided to turn around." Hugh's response was childish; he knew it as he said it.

Alice's parasol caught on a branch hanging over the narrowing road. She shrieked as she tried to keep hold of it. The lace tore with a terrible, audible rip.

"This is a brand-new parasol!" Alice cried. She regarded the fresh hole in dismay. Just as Hugh was putting together an apology, she whacked him with what remained. "Turn us around! Turn us around right now!"

He was so startled at the hit that he dropped the reins. The horses, surprised by the sudden looseness, accelerated into a trot. Yanking the whalebone handle from Alice's grasp, Hugh held the parasol in one hand and reached for the leather straps before they were lost between the horses' legs. He only managed to grab the right, which sent the horses into a hard turn to the left. The barouche careened, nearly tilting onto only the left wheels, before smashing on Alice's side into a tree.

The horses stopped. The carriage still rattled. Hugh grabbed Alice in both hands. "Are you all right?"

Alice blinked up at him for a moment. Long enough for Hugh to assess that she had not been damaged. Then she started hitting him again, this time with nothing but her hands. She hit his chest, his arms, his legs. Anything she could reach. She cried out, too, but Hugh couldn't understand what she said. Only what she meant:

How could he?

He didn't know how to stop her. He didn't know how to calm her. He kept his hands on either shoulder, but she kept hitting him. Tears were welling in her eyes now. Hugh wanted to stop the storm before she hyperventilated.

So, he did the only thing he could think of.

He kissed her.

At first, she was frozen in surprise. Hugh wrapped both arms around her torso as he pillowed his lips against hers. Today she smelled of lilac and vanilla.

Then, Alice joined him in the kiss. Her hands twisted around his neck. Long fingers reached into his hair. Hugh's grip on her tightened, and in response she climbed into his lap. Her muslin dress and petticoats hiked around her knees as she straddled him. Hugh explored her jaw with fluttering kisses as his hands traveled down to her legs, bare save for her stockings.

Then his eyes slid over her chest. From behind the thin curtain of her bodice, Alice's nipples stood round and erect. If Hugh wanted to, he could dot them with precise kisses. And he wanted to. He scooped downwards, pressing through her gown with his tongue. Alice let out a little moan, and his groin grew hotter, tighter. Hugh ran his thumb under the rim of her neckline, scooping now to brush the pad of his finger against her peak. Alice slammed a palm against the back of the barouche, bracing herself, and Hugh glanced up at her eyes. They were dark and green and begging for more. Keeping their gaze, he slid his whole palm under her neckline until her breasts were free of her dress.

How exquisite they were: rosy and pert and just the size to fit in his palm. Hugh pulled Alice ever closer, teasing her breasts with kisses and whispers of breath. She was hot everywhere he touched her. Her free fingers pulled against his hair as he played, tugging as he aroused her more and more.

Hugh knew he should bring it to a stop. But he couldn't resist; as Alice moaned again at his kiss on her breast, he slid his fingers up her thigh until he found her hot, wet folds. Alice hissed, and suddenly he was harder than he'd ever been in his life.

He explored the length of her heat, then started lazy circles around her ever-growing mound. Alice was completely still in his arms. Hugh risked another glance up to her eyes and found them glazed with desire. He paused, just for a second, and she whispered, "Don't stop whatever you're doing."

And so, he sped it up. Circling closer and closer. Watching her eyes darken. Listening to her breath shorten. When he didn't think she could take any more, he hurried it into a frenzy and pressed a kiss into her breast. He wanted to consume her. He wanted to fit himself against her and hold her like that forever. But he would settle for this: her loud, throaty cry of delight as he caressed her into oblivion.

Alice collapsed into him. Hugh held her close as she trembled from the aftereffects. He limited himself to one tender kiss to her cheek. These weren't kisses of desire; they were kisses of love, and he had to be careful not to dole out too many, knowing he wouldn't get any back. So, he kissed her cheek the once, and then he hugged her against him for as long as she needed, staring at the cloudy English sky to memorize the moment.

Chapter Twenty-Two

Alice was made of jelly. She was made of jelly, and nothing mattered except the very physical, heady sensation that she'd just been shown the center of the universe. And it was between her legs.

Slowly, she returned to the rest of her body. Her feet, dangling off the edge of the barouche bench. Her hands, cradling the back of Hugh's neck. Her breasts, still bare, scratching against the wool of his coat. Her head, paired against his, as if they were two lovers.

Which in a way, she supposed, they were.

Straightening, Alice knew she should probably be embarrassed about what had just happened. Hugh had seen her breasts. He had fondled her in a place even she had never touched.

But it had felt so good. It had felt so right. He hadn't even fondled her: it had all been caresses. And it had serviced such an amazing, indescribable experience.

An experience, she supposed, that was usually saved for the wedding night. Fixing her bodice, she returned to her own seat and tried to sound wry as she asked, "Am I quite ruined now?"

Hugh smiled. He was handsome when he looked so free of worries. "Not quite. Just a little further along the road."

Seeing as he didn't have a problem with it, Alice supposed she needn't feel guilty. As long as it was just the two of them that knew.

"What do we do now?" she asked.

Hugh sat up, as if noticing the mess that was their barouche for the first time. The right-hand wheel, which had crashed into the tree, stood at an awkward angle. Alice doubted it would turn if they tried it. Meanwhile, the horses huffed impatiently, each one stuck between a different tree on the other side of the narrow path.

They were most definitely not on the right road.

Yet Alice couldn't seem to summon the same anger that had driven her to start hitting Hugh. In fact, at the moment, the whole thing seemed quite funny.

"We had better get to the races, or the whole *ton* will think I've taken advantage." Hugh winked at her. Alice giggled. She'd never known a wink could feel so wonderfully intimate.

"I suppose we'll have to unhitch the horses and walk with them to the nearest blacksmith or inn, where perhaps we can borrow another carriage or saddles." Hugh cut an uncertain look to her. "Are you able to walk?"

"I'm not an invalid," Alice protested. "Walking is one of my favorite pastimes at Bleneccle Manor."

Hugh raised a single eyebrow in challenge. "Of course, that's precisely what you said when we walked at the Serpentine."

Descending from the carriage, he offered a hand to

help her down. She picked up her poor, tattered parasol from the floor of the barouche. Hugh winced. "I do apologize about that. I'll buy you a new one."

Alice hadn't particularly liked the lace pattern anyhow. Lady Eastley had chosen it during their latest trousseau shopping trip, and Alice hadn't cared enough to argue. But she didn't need to let Hugh know that. "You'll buy me two new ones, as penance for your pigheadedness."

He tilted his head to accept the terms.

Each leading a horse, they left the barouche behind and made their way on foot back along the path. It was eerily quiet now that Alice was accustomed to the bustle of London. She hadn't been amongst so many trees since she'd left Bleneccle Manor. She'd forgotten how loudly birds trilled to each other amongst the branches. All in all, it was a lovely afternoon to be caught in a forest.

She glanced over at her companion. She'd admired his build before, the sinews of his arms and shape of his legs. But now she knew the muscular energy bundled beneath his coat. She'd buttressed her own thighs against his. She'd even felt his manhood, strong and proud beneath his linen britches.

And now she knew the secret power of his fingers, which before had seemed ordinarily solid.

"Have you done that before?" she asked, shocking herself with the question. "You seemed to know what you were doing."

Hugh immediately blushed a bright, beet red. Alice rather enjoyed that. She could have been referencing anything, but clearly Hugh's mind was on the same track as hers. He cleared his throat. "Yes."

"With whom?" This she really shouldn't ask. Margot had as much as warned Alice that men learned the tricks of the bedroom from harlots and loose women. A wife did not want nor need to know more.

But Alice did. She couldn't picture timid Hugh seeking out a harlot, nor could she see him seducing some poor bar wench. Yet somehow, here he was. With magic hands.

"Do you really want to know?" Hugh asked.

"I wouldn't ask otherwise."

He was quiet for a few more steps. The birds sang happily through the sky.

Alice prodded, "Was it at Cambridge? I've heard universities are actually quite debauched."

"For other students, yes. For me, I was always much too obsessed with my studies to be distracted." Hugh blushed again. "A widow in the village near Richmond Hall befriended me. I suppose she was bored."

Alice immediately tried to remember all the widows she'd ever heard of around Richmond Hall. There were plenty: it could have been any old sailor's widow, or a soldier's widow, or perhaps the parson's widow. Suddenly, she wasn't sure she wanted to know.

"She has since remarried," Hugh added, "and I believe they relocated to her husband's home parish near Bath."

That was clear across the country. Alice exhaled in relief. "Well, I owe her a debt of gratitude."

Hugh grinned. He walked a few paces, then asked, "What of you? When was your first kiss?"

A perfectly good way to ruin the mood. "I believe you witnessed it yourself."

Hugh's horse jerked as he swung around for a better look at her. "*That* was your first kiss?"

Alice straightened her shoulders. "Why should that be so shocking? I am a well-bred young lady."

"Yes, a well-bred young lady who has been nothing but forward with me."

She smiled; she couldn't regret where forwardness had gotten them today. "You're my intended. I thought you liked my forwardness."

"I do. I only assumed you'd had more practice." Hugh looked thoughtfully down at the ground. "And it makes Cornwall's behavior all the more abrasive."

Alice didn't want to comment on that. She was through with thinking of the Duke of Cornwall.

They walked further in amicable silence. Alice's mind wandered into the future, to when they might be walking their own estate in similar comfortable friendship, when Hugh said, "I do regret that you felt so attacked by Lady Windemere. I suppose I am so used to her manner that I forget how brusque it can feel if you are not."

Alice wished he hadn't brought it up again. She'd rather the friendly quiet than another rehash of something they clearly didn't see eye-to-eye on. Still, it was the closest he'd gotten to apologizing.

"Usually, she is at her most abrasive when she cares most about the subject. When my latest sister passed, Lady Windemere told me I was an idiot for crying, since we should all know by now that her daughters did nothing but die."

The traces of the hurt that caused were evident in how Hugh said this with a humorless smile and in the slight ball of his fist. His horse knickered.

"In this case," Hugh continued, "she knows of my... fondness for you. And given the circumstances, she assumes it is one-sided. If you can put yourself in her shoes, you might see how she would desire to communicate with you about this."

Alice wouldn't use the word *communicate* to describe what Lady Windemere had been attempting to do. *Humiliate* was more like it. But she bit back her ire, harnessing the goodwill they'd established to try to do as Hugh recommended and put herself in the countess's perspective.

She supposed she would want to know that the young lady in question would at least try to reciprocate her son's feelings.

But that wasn't what Lady Windemere had been on about, was it? She wanted Alice to admit her wanton ways. She wanted to drag Alice's name through the mud. She didn't want them to have a happy marriage. Lady Windemere wanted to sabotage it.

And Hugh would let her.

As if reading her mind, Hugh added, "I suppose you are also right that I should remind my mother of manners. However, the meat of what I've been trying to express, is that for me, this really isn't about my mother. If you style yourself as caring about me at all, I would appreciate if you would try to assuage her concerns."

"Perhaps if I go in now, knowing what to expect, I will have the stomach for it," Alice ventured.

Hugh smiled. "How about this: if you promise to be civil and stay for only a quarter hour, I'll get my mother to promise to be civil."

"You have a deal."

They settled back into their comfortable silence. The main road was now on the horizon, where the trees grew wider apart and Alice could spot a carriage rolling by every now and then. Soon, they would be back on track for the horse race.

*If you style yourself as caring about me...*what on earth could he mean by that? Was that why he was so upset about it all? Alice had thought Hugh was simply so much under his mother's wing that he couldn't stand her to insult Lady Windemere. Was he saying this was actually all about his wounded heart?

More to the point, did he really think that Alice only *styled* herself as caring about him? Of course, she had been terrible to him at the start of their engagement, but she had apologized about it. Though now that Alice thought of it, she realized that immediately after apologizing, she had frozen Lady Windemere with silence. If she were Hugh, without access to Alice's heart and mind, she could see why he might think she was only pretending to care.

The reality was that she'd spent the last week growing more and more distracted by Hugh. It had started with her determination to forget the Duke of Cornwall. Whenever she daydreamed of Alan, she replaced him with Hugh. But it hadn't taken much effort. After all, her entire month was dedicated to preparing for wedding Hugh. All anyone spoke about was their marriage; all she did was shop for a trousseau that would outfit her for their life together. She'd grown fond of imagining Hugh's little smiles in reaction to this dress or that riding habit; at the glove store, she pictured him plucking them from her fingers one at a time; it was why she hadn't liked that parasol, because she couldn't come up with how Hugh would react to it.

Even in her anger for the past day, Alice couldn't stop thinking about Hugh. She imagined him storming into their supper to demand an apology. She couldn't sleep for dreaming of him throwing rocks at her window, to beckon her down to the garden so he could admit how wrong he was. Up until the moment he'd shown up in person to collect her on the barouche, Alice had ached for him to return, so she could find out what he would do next.

But Hugh didn't know any of this. And Alice didn't

know how to tell him.

They found a blacksmith not far along the main road, who sent a boy to fetch them a hackney coach. Hugh passed the time interrogating the smith on his various tools. He fairly lit up whenever he was around iron, Alice discovered. He wanted to try out the hammers; he weighed the horseshoes in his palms; he even tried out the anvil, face bursting red at the effort. He returned to Alice as delighted as a boy in a candy store.

"Quite fascinating, isn't it?"

She nodded, though of course she was more fascinated by him than by the anvil.

Perhaps too fascinated.

The hackney was a little old and dirty, but it would do the trick. Alice was disappointed to find it had two benches, as that meant Hugh would sit opposite her rather than snugly at her side. In fact, it was so spacious that her skirt didn't even brush Hugh's leg.

Probably for the best, considering how carried away they'd gotten earlier. Still, Alice longed to feel his body heat again. And perhaps next time, she wouldn't be the only one in a state of undress.

The regatta was well underway by the time they got there, though there were other carriages just now arriving. Alice gave her dress one last check – after all, it had gotten quite mussed – before accepting Hugh's awaiting hand to alight.

Lady Eastley rushed to their side. "There you are! I

was beginning to worry."

Hugh bowed in greeting. "The fault is mine, Lady Eastley. I am embarrassed to admit that I lost control of the curricle, and we found ourselves on foot for a good part of the journey. Luckily, your daughter is just as delightful walking as she is when properly transported."

Alice felt her mother's eyes raking over her, checking for damage. Alice met Lady Eastley's gaze with a smile. "It was quite the adventure, but we were never in danger. How goes the racing?"

"I haven't even gotten to the races yet," Lady Eastley admitted. "Come, I have a throng of admirers who want to congratulate the two of you."

She led them to the great lawn, where most of the attendees were gathered in clumps or sitting on benches. They had a view of the racetrack, but no one watched the horses. All eyes were on who was there, who was being scandalous, and who was not.

True to her word, Lady Eastley had found all sorts of people to introduce Alice to that hadn't yet congratulated her on the engagement. She met the Earls of Orange, Rutherford, and Rutland; Lords Farraway and Cumberland; Misters Uxley and Babish; the Dukes of Devonshire and Hampshire. Of course, each of the gentlemen was accompanied by a wife. Alice found herself constantly bobbing in and out of a curtsy and caught in an endless cycle of small talk.

They were all in a clump, chatting merrily away. Alice's eyes were on Lady Cumberland as they discussed the upcoming opera, so there was no reason that she should have noticed him approaching. But she did. She was the first one to see him, out of the corner of her eye – a hulking, dark figure walking straight for their group.

The Duke of Cornwall.

She determined in that moment that he would not fluster her. Alan – no, he was back to *His Grace, Duke of Cornwall* – no longer held any power over her. He was simply another lord.

Beside her, Hugh stiffened. Alice longed to put her hand in his and squeeze it tight. Instead, she merely took a small, tiny step closer to him.

"Good day," the duke said, joining the group.

"Cornwall, excellent," the Duke of Devonshire said. "I've been looking for you. What's your bet: Blue Vixen or Sassafras?"

"Blue Vixen, of course."

He wasn't as handsome as Alice remembered. For one, she'd built him up in her head to be seven feet tall, when really he was only a few inches higher than the Duke of Devonshire. For another, his whole face was rather dark and sallow, the picture of a man who spent too much time out and about at night. And those sharp cheekbones she had so exulted were actually rather off-putting. She couldn't imagine resting her own face against his, the way she had with Hugh just an hour or two earlier.

The dukes bantered about the bet for a little while

longer. Then the Duke of Cornwall turned to the Earl of Rutherford. "I beg your pardon, but could I steal you away for a moment?"

The earl, of course, consented. It would have been perfectly polite for the duke to bid the group farewell with a general nod of his head, or a "Good afternoon" not directed at any one person in particular.

But that did not suit him. Instead, the Duke of Cornwall turned to each person individually. "Good afternoon, Lady Rutherford. Good afternoon, Lord Farraway. Good afternoon, Lady Farraway." And so on, and so forth. Alice's stomach tightened each time his head nodded. His eyes slid like a snake from one person to another. And she knew what poison this snake meant to release.

Alice flinched when the duke reached her mother, but the Duke of Cornwall didn't miss a beat. "Good afternoon, Lady Eastley."

Alice grimaced when he got to Hugh. But despite a slight curl to his lips, the duke still spit out, "Good afternoon, Lord Windemere."

No, it was only once he reached Alice that her premonition came true. His eyes snaked directly over her. As if she didn't exist. And his next words were not for her, but for Lady Cumberland beside her.

He had cut her direct. Again.

On the far side of the clump, Lady Farraway gasped. Other than that, no one acknowledged what had happened. When the duke had finally finished saying his farewell, he and the Earl of Rutherford walked off as if nothing was out of sorts.

And their group was left in silence.

Alice's cheeks burned, though she had vowed not to let him under her skin. So what, if he cut her direct? She didn't want to speak to him anyway. This way, they didn't need to pretend there was any good will between them. It was better all around.

But it made her look like *she* was in the wrong. As far as Society knew, one minute Alice was the Duke of Cornwall's favorite dance partner, and the next, she was engaged to Hugh and given the cut direct.

They didn't have any idea he was the one who had taken advantage of her.

Alice waited. Someone would startle the group out of their silence. It couldn't be her. If she had patience, someone would speak so that Alice wouldn't burn in humiliation any longer.

Someone *had* to, otherwise Alice was quite convinced the ground would open up and swallow her whole.

And someone did. The last person she expected: her very own Hugh. He turned to the Duchess of Hampshire. "Do you know, Your Grace, I don't believe there has ever been a bridegroom as excited as I? Lady Windemere commented a few days ago she has never seen me smile as much as I have since Miss Winpole accepted my offer."

The words alone brought tears to Alice's eyes. The earnestness on Hugh's face – so different than the boredom with which the Duke of Cornwall effected his blow – made her heart thrum.

And evidently, those two factors convinced the duchess that Hugh spoke truth. "A lucky lady, indeed, to have so passionate a bridegroom."

The Duke of Hampshire raised his monocle to his eye and examined Alice. "Indeed. Miss Winpole, perhaps you will save a dance for me at the ball this evening, so I may learn how you have delighted our Lord Windemere."

"I should be honored," Alice said, blushing, even as the Duke of Devonshire threw his cap into the ring as well.

They might as well have been throwing an obscene gesture the Duke of Cornwall's way. In just the dance offers alone, Alice was redeemed from her cut direct.

And it was all because Hugh dared speak up.

No, she didn't *style* herself to care about him. She cared about him, more and more every day.

It was about time she proved it to him.

Chapter Twenty-Three

"The last time I saw you, you were nothing but a long face about your marriage, and now you're glowing!"

Lisbeth said this as she stole Alice away for a sojourn to her father's library. Lady Eastley and Alice had finally found time to pay a call to the Dawes house once more, and Alice was determined to fill Lisbeth in on everything.

Well, save the most intimate details. Alice wasn't quite sure she wanted to tell even her best friend about the magic spell Hugh had cast on her body in the curricle.

They nestled onto a settee near one of the library's great windows overlooking the square. "There's a great deal I haven't been able to tell you yet," Alice prefaced before launching into the full explanation: Lady Windemere's warning, the duke's advances in the garden, Hugh's proposal, Alice's own capriciousness. "I have treated him horridly and yet he still wants to marry me. He's been sending me gifts every day."

Alice held out her wrist, which featured a fresh posy of roses that Hugh had sent that very morning.

Lisbeth cooed over it. She herself sported a violet in her hair. Alice leaned forward. "What of you? Is that violet from an admirer?"

Lisbeth's hand flew to the flower in question. "Lord

Gresham sent his compliments."

"It looks as if you're happy to receive his compliments."

There was the briefest of pauses. Alice recognized it from her own retinue of hesitations. As much as one wanted an admirer, once one was acquired, it really was confusing.

Lisbeth donned a smile. Her brown eyes were good at masking her emotions, except Alice already knew her too well. "What's not to like? He has a charming smile and a good fortune. I could do much worse."

Alice took her friend's hand as she echoed back the question. "So, what's not to like?"

"It's silly."

"It can't be as silly as the story I just told you," Alice wheedled.

Lisbeth let out a wicked snort. "True. I haven't been nearly as silly as you." She looked down to her lap to gather her words. "For all that Lord Gresham is handsome and well-bred, I find him rather…boring. He only ever seems interested in the weather or horses."

Alice had danced once with Lord Gresham, and she did recall that the conversation had centered on whether or not it would rain the next day.

"How dreary."

"Exactly. I always imagined my husband would be overly intelligent, with a keen interest at least in politics." Lisbeth looked wistfully at her father's bookshelves.

"I suppose it's a small tradeoff to a good marriage, and with someone who doesn't smell too terribly to boot."

Alice tried to find something optimistic for her friend. "Perhaps he's saving his interesting conversation for when you are more intimate."

"Perhaps." Lisbeth returned her warm brown gaze to Alice. "Now that all is said and done, are you glad that things worked out the way they did? So you can marry Lord Windemere?"

Just the mere mention of Hugh warmed Alice's heart. It had been in this very library that she had first touched him, her bare finger to his soft, chestnut hair. Alice's heart tripped a little, looking forward to Sunday, when she would see him next.

"I certainly wish the events had been arranged differently," Alice allowed, "but yes, I am happy to be marrying Lord Windemere."

How different it would be to feel like Lisbeth, settling for a husband who might bore her to death.

How lucky Alice was to have finally recognized that Hugh was the best husband for her.

Lisbeth wrapped Alice's palm in hers. "Then I'm happy for you. I expect you shall have nothing but wedded bliss."

Alice agreed. There was no reason theirs would be anything but a blissful marriage.

Chapter Twenty-Four

The closer the wedding approached, the slower time seemed to go. Alice didn't see enough of Hugh, though he was marvelous about sending little tokens each day. Some days it was flowers, some days it was chocolates; on Friday it had even been a set of books on mechanics. Alice sent back a note each day, telling him how she delighted in each particular gift.

The flowers stand on my windowsill to greet me, so my first thought each morning is of you.

I have eaten all the chocolates, though I wish I could share them with you.

I shall endeavor to read the whole set before our wedding, though undoubtedly it will mean no sleeping or socializing, so that you can spend our honeymoon showing me the intricacies of your machines.

Still, knowing she was in his thoughts wasn't the same as being near to Hugh. At church that week, he invited all of them – even Margot and her husband – to sit with him in his pew. Alice was between her parents, but she could smell Hugh. They kept sneaking peeks at each other, which of course resulted in little smiles and laughs that were entirely out of place for the sermon on grief.

After the service, it seemed a hundred people had something to say. Alice thought Hugh would never ask if he could take her home for tea with Lady Windemere. But finally, he did, with a slight bow to Lord Eastley, who chuckled. "Don't keep her too long. We've only a few days left with her before you take her off forever."

"We will be frequent visitors at Bleneccle Manor, of course," Hugh promised, offering Alice his arm.

She trembled a little at that first touch. She'd forgotten how heavenly it was to stand beside him. Alice did her best to look pure and innocent as they traipsed down the cathedral steps into his waiting carriage. She lasted until they had pulled out of sight of the church to jump to his side of the bench.

"Is this the behavior of a well-bred lady?" Hugh asked, in the same breath as cupping her cheeks in both hands and landing a delicious kiss on her lips. "I have missed you."

Alice braced a hand on his thigh as the carriage jostled. "Thank you for all the gifts. I feel quite spoiled."

"You might want to move your hand, or you really will be spoiled before our wedding night."

Alice did, but only so she could thread her gloved fingers through his hair. It was so wonderfully thick and smooth. Perfect for gripping while she hungered for him with her lips, inhaling the scent of his cologne mixed with oil from his machines. Hugh's hand tickled across her breast, the softest of touches, and she gasped with pleasure, remembering where that had taken them previously.

"Perhaps we had better behave ourselves on a Sunday," Hugh whispered, as his fingers wickedly raced down her waist.

Alice captured his earlobe between her lips, on impulse, and his breath caught. He returned her mouth to his and kissed her greedily. Alice's body grew hot in response, and that magic spot he'd so expertly greeted went instantly wet. She moved to climb onto his lap again.

Hugh pulled back. "Really, Alice, I should hate to arrive for tea in a state."

Pouting, Alice sat back. She'd managed to forget the fact they were off for round two of tea with Lady Windemere. He was probably right: she didn't want to show up looking like the harlot she was. But how Alice wanted to find out what came next.

"Perhaps when I escort you home, we can take the long way," Hugh whispered.

Alice grinned.

They arrived to the Osborne house all too soon for Alice's preference. Her stomach flipped at the mere sight of it and the specter of the lady that awaited her inside.

Hugh squeezed her hand as he helped her onto the front stairs. "You are going to delight her."

Alice had no hope of that. But she did hope to show Lady Windemere – and more importantly, Hugh – that she truly cared for him.

Alby showed them to the drawing room, whose curtains were once again drawn closed. "Would you like me to fetch her ladyship?"

Hugh squeezed Alice's hand once more. "I'll do it. I'd like to make sure she is in the right state of mind before she descends."

Alice listened to his footfalls as he climbed the stairs. There was a bounce to his step, and she suspected she was the reason. It was thrilling to know he smiled when she looked at him.

Or that she smiled because he looked at her.

Alice didn't want to say anything to him yet, because she wasn't quite sure, but she suspected that somewhere between their broken curricle ride and the week of flurried gifts, she had fallen in love with her fiancé.

Lady Windemere's strident voice carried down from the second floor. Alice shuddered. *You're making a bigger deal of it than it is*, she scolded herself. *Whoever was scared of an old lady?*

Still, with her whole body squeezing in fear, Alice supposed she had better find the water closet before it was too late. Slipping out of the sitting room, she wandered down the hall to the little room near the service door in the back of the townhouse.

It was a dark closet with ugly brown wallpaper that made Alice think of a hunt. She was in the middle of dreaming up how she'd redecorate it – creamy light colors and lavender sachets – when Alice realized she could hear Lady Windemere as if in the same room.

"I will be perfectly pleasant, as always. I do not need

my son to tell me how to be a lady."

The water closet must have been situated directly under Lady Windemere's quarters. The countess spoke so loudly, her words carried downwards through the innards of the house as easily as across.

Finished with her business, Alice neatened up, to give herself a pretense to keep listening. Though the more Lady Windemere said, the less Alice wanted to hear.

"It's too late for me to do anything now even if I wanted to. Only a week from the wedding. The tongues would wag worse if I tried to stop it."

Alice couldn't hear Hugh's replies as easily, only the muffled depth of his voice.

"I know it was my plan to begin with for you to marry little Miss Winpole, but now I wish we'd let Cornwall take her when he wanted to."

A bucket of cold water might as well have been dumped over Alice's head. She couldn't breathe, could barely even see.

It really *had* been a plan all along.

Osborne must have his way.

The Duke of Cornwall must truly have wanted to marry Alice. Had Lady Windemere stopped it somehow? Was that why he cut Alice after that bewildering visit on the balcony – because Lady Windemere made him?

Suddenly, Alice remembered that poor housekeeper in Cumbria, turned out without reference or pay because Lady Windemere had orchestrated to find her in a ruinous position.

Alice was only her latest victim.

Alice pushed out of the water closet blindly. Hugh may not have even known about the plan. Lady Windemere was nasty and clever enough to master it from her bedroom. He was likely a pawn, unaware of his own mother's machinations.

Unaware that she was ruining lives.

Alby stepped out of Alice's way as she barreled down the hall. "May I help you, my lady?"

"Yes. Get me a hackney." Alice had never traveled through London alone. It was wildly indecent, but then, that was what she was fast becoming. An indecent, loose, unmarried woman.

All because Lady Windemere wanted it that way.

The butler hesitated. Alice stormed past him. "Never mind, I'll do it myself."

"Alice, where are you going?" Hugh's voice came from the top landing of the stairs. He had his mother in a chair and a footman to help him carry her down.

Oh, but he was beautiful. Alice wished she'd never set eyes on him, so she didn't know the pain of saying goodbye.

"I will have no part of a family that plots to ruin a young lady just to trap her into marriage. If you don't know of what I speak, ask Lady Windemere."

Alby had his hand on the front door, but Alice yanked it open anyway. She took one last glare at Lady Windemere, whose eyes glowed from her sick chair, before tearing into the London streets.

Chapter Twenty-Five

Hugh was not one for gentlemen's clubs. In fact, he'd never been to one before. He only had a membership at White's because he'd inherited it from his father. It was one of those dues paid yearly by his steward.

Before that night, Hugh had never had any interest in drinking, or smoking, or chatting, or any of the activities he understood to take place in a club.

But Miss Alice Winpole had done a number on him. After she'd raced out of his house – quite literally running, in her Sunday best, down their Mayfair street – she'd refused to speak to him. Even after he caught up to her. Even after he insisted they get in a hackney. Even after he escorted her inside her home and explained in plain English to Lord Eastley that he had no idea what was wrong.

It was the Alice who had started their engagement: stony and silent and angry. Only she didn't respond to any of his questions or prompts. He reached out to take her hand, hoping physical touch might jostle her out of her fugue, but she leapt away from him, nearly out of the carriage.

Lord Eastley had watched her race up the staircase, then shrugged. "Overly excited, I'd guess. Don't take it personally. She'll be back to her cheerful old self by wedding day."

Only Hugh wasn't certain Alice intended for there to be a wedding day. *I will have no part of a family...*

"Do you have the slightest idea what she was talking about?" he asked his mother on return.

Lady Windemere didn't. "Something set her off, and we'll never know what it was. The best thing now is to let her cool down. I'll send a note to Lady Eastley."

Hugh sent a note, too. One for Lady Eastley, one for Lady Wickham, and one for Alice.

I don't know what happened. I hate to see you upset. I want to make it right. I love you, and always will.

After that, he tried to distract himself with the workshop. But his machine wasn't working, and for once, he didn't have the concentration to fix it. Every other thought was of Alice.

Nor did he have the appetite for supper. And he certainly couldn't just sit at home, staring at the wall, waiting for a message from Alice.

So here he was. At the club. With the other men hiding from their women.

For the most part, it wasn't too bad. Hugh burned his bad feeling with a glass of fine Scotch whiskey and got into a discussion on the merits of reforming the Bloody Code with Lord Pemberly. He even found enough of an appetite to order a cut of roast beef and mashed potatoes.

Alice will calm down, he decided. *It's not as if I did*

anything to cause her offense.

He was fairly certain that was true. In the carriage from church, she'd been anything but angry with him. Even if she'd been put out that he delayed their amorousness, Alice hadn't seemed upset when he left her in the sitting room.

Between that moment and her slamming the door on the way out, all he'd done was go collect his mother. It was true that Lady Windemere had been in a bit of a mood. She hadn't been feeling well all day and hardly saw the point of tea, since Alice was going to be living in the same house soon.

I will have no part of a family that plots to ruin a young lady just to trap her into marriage.

Had Alice somehow heard his mother going on about the Duke of Cornwall?

Hugh's stomach twisted. That must have been it. He didn't know how she could have heard from the sitting room, but she must have done. And misunderstood. She'd always believed there was some ugly reason why the duke had left her high and dry.

What was it his mother had said? *I wish we'd let Cornwall take her when he wanted to.*

Hugh had scoffed when she said it. As if they'd had any control over Cornwall's actions. But if Alice had heard that — and believed his mother in touch with reality — well, she would have run out with an angry slam of the door.

Alice was never going to marry him now.

"Ah, here comes your rival," Pemberly said, returning Hugh to the smoky environs of the club. "I heard he gave Miss Winpole the cut direct at the horse races. He must be sore at losing her to you."

Hugh followed Pemberly's gaze to see Cornwall entering from the gaming room. The other gentlemen instinctually drew away as he stalked through the chairs. One didn't have to know him to sense that he was a predator.

Hugh would not reward Cornwall with attention. He turned back to Pemberly. "He is a puzzling man. Why he didn't offer for Miss Winpole, I'll never know. I only count my lucky stars he didn't, since otherwise I wouldn't have stood a chance."

A big, meaty hand clamped on Hugh's shoulder. "That's absolutely right, Windemere. You never stand a chance in a competition with me."

Cornwall's words slurred; he was more than a little over the edge of consumption. Hugh stood to free himself of the man's hand. The very hand that had once groped at Alice in the garden.

"Cornwall, answer me something." Pemberly sat back in his chair, eyes twinkling as he regarded the two men in front of him. "If you're so upset that Windemere ended up with the lucky Miss Winpole, why didn't you offer for her yourself?

The duke waved his hand as if swatting away a fly.

"I'm not upset. I'm lucky. I wouldn't offer marriage to that hussy if the king himself ordered me to. She's loose. Out to trap a husband. My pity to Windemere here for falling into it."

Hugh's fingers curled into a fist. How he wanted to swing it straight for Cornwall's mouth, wipe those words off his lips. But he was no idiot. He didn't stand a chance in a fistfight with Cornwall. And given their longstanding hatred for each other, no doubt Cornwall would take the opportunity to pummel him to death.

"That is a lady's honor you disparage. Rescind your words."

Cornwall only looked at him with drunken black eyes.

"Rescind your words, Your Grace." The whole club was silent by now, watching the standoff.

"I will do the opposite. I will say it more clearly. Miss Winpole is a loose woman, not worthy of any peer."

Hugh's rage was so strong, he felt as tall as a horse. He fairly spat his next words. "I demand satisfaction."

Cornwall curled back his lip in a happy snarl. "The pleasure is mine, Lord Windemere. But let's not wait a whole day. This morning at dawn. Battersea Fields."

He turned on his heel, not waiting for Hugh to name his seconds or object to the unusual protocol. Hugh didn't care. The sooner, the better.

His heart hammered strong and true until the duke was out of sight.

Then it started rattling.

Pemberly patted his back. "I'm sorry I asked the question. I meant it in jest, of course."

Hugh nodded.

He was a realistic man. He'd spent his life learning how machines worked, not practicing his shots. And Cornwall had spent his life shooting on the battlefield. When not harboring his strange hatred for Hugh.

Hugh had a few hours left of living. Then, likely, Cornwall would put a bullet straight through his heart.

Chapter Twenty-Six

Alice had stayed up until dawn a handful of times in her life. At midsummer at Bleneccle Manor. The evening Geoff offered for Margot, when the two sisters whispered together all night in Margot's bed. And of course, several times this Season, as the carriages rolled home from the balls.

Never before had she held vigil simply to argue with her family.

Yet argue seemed to be all they could do. The moment she had returned home – just as she had flung herself across her bed, ready to sob the feelings out of herself – her father stormed into her room.

"Just what do you think you're doing, running across London by yourself? Making a spectacle of your honor and this family name?"

Alice was so shocked to see her father in her bedroom that she could only stare.

"You're about to have a good marriage, despite your unladylike behavior. Lord Windemere is most distressed with you this afternoon. You will write him a note in apology. Now."

"My unladylike behavior? You told me the duke was going to offer for me. You wanted me to go into the garden!"

Lord Eastley, red in the face, deflated. He was a man

of bluster: he got angry quickly, and that anger disappeared just as fast. He moved to the settee at the end of Alice's bed. "That's all in the past. Or at least it will be. If you can just calm your nerves and see through the next few days."

Alice's heart split in two again. That horrible Lady Windemere. If it weren't for her schemes, Alice could still marry Hugh. But she couldn't live in the same house as a woman who thought she could play puppet master to the world.

"Did Lord Windemere offend you?" her father asked. "Is that why you're upset?"

She shook her head.

"He'll be a good husband to you. Honor be damned; I wouldn't have agreed to his offer if I didn't think he'd be a good husband to you."

And he would have, too. Alice knew that. Hugh with his serious way of examining every detail before making a decision. His solid interest in improving the world around him. His devotion to her. She would have loved to be his wife.

A sob threatened to wrench her whole body.

"Won't you tell me what is bothering you, Alice?" Lord Eastley stretched out a hand, clearly wanting her to take his.

But Alice could only throw herself to her pillows. "I can't marry Lord Windemere."

After that, her father marshalled Lady Eastley, followed by Margot. Alice spent most of the afternoon too distraught to string words together, trying to get them to leave her alone. "I'll explain everything if only you'll let me have a few minutes of quiet."

She needed to whip her own thoughts into clarity before she had to explain herself. She wanted to purge her heart of tenderness for Hugh before she had to defend her decision.

Because despite her misery, Alice knew without a doubt one thing: she would not marry a man whose mother had planned her dishonor.

Even if it meant she ended up in the poorhouse.

They let her alone for supper, or rather, Margot was Alice's only supper companion up in her bedroom, and Margot was wise enough to leave the subject while they ate. She instead focused on cajoling Alice into eating more of the broth Cook had sent up. "If you don't eat, you won't have the energy to hold your ground, whatever your ground is."

"My ground is Antarctica. Unbreachable."

Margot measured her with a soft gaze. "That sounds cold. All the more reason to eat up."

The food did help. It made her feel whole again, instead of like some rag riddled with holes that Lady Windemere had thrown into the gutter. Alice changed into a more comfortable morning gown, splashed some water on her face, and descended to the sitting room for a proper chat with her family.

They were the picture of a quiet Sunday night: Mother by the fire with her embroidery, Father palming a goblet of amber brandy, Margot rifling through the pages of a book. Except it was the Season. They were likely supposed to be at someone's fancy dinner. Margot was meant to be with her own family.

And Alice should have been enjoying a few final nights of maidenhood.

She chose her words carefully to begin, striving to sound the part of a mature lady who knew exactly what she was doing. "I apologize for the to-do I've caused. I really don't mean to cause any distress. Unfortunately, the circumstances dictate that it must be so."

Her family stayed quiet, waiting for her to go on.

"As you know, this whole mess started when I agreed to walk in the garden with the Duke of Cornwall. We all believed he had expressed so much interest in me that he was going to offer. I dared think he might ask for my hand in the garden. When he instead got amorous..." This was difficult to speak of to any audience, let alone her parents. Alice's skin scalded with a blush, but she pressed on. "I suppose I thought it was just another sign that an offer was coming. I believe we all thought that, until the moment he simply walked off.

"I have never been able to understand that moment. He was so kind to me before and so complimentary. I wasn't the one who suggested a walk in the garden, nor was I the one to initiate...amorousness. So why did he accuse me of trying to trap him? Why did he risk his own honor in order to not marry me?

"Meanwhile, Lady Windemere had left her sickbed to warn us that if we weren't careful with the Duke of Cornwall, he would do something dishonorable. She said Lord Windemere would keep an eye on me, as if I needed an extra chaperone. And indeed, he sought me out from that moment onward. He also warned me against the duke. And, most strange, he was one of the group that discovered us in that compromising position.

"I have long felt that some external plot must have forced the Duke of Cornwall to behave so dishonorably. This afternoon, I overheard Lady Windemere confirm my suspicions. She said, *We should have let Cornwall marry her when he wanted to.*"

Alice paused, watching her parents' faces for reactions. Lady Eastley was, for the most part, impassive, while Lord Eastley frowned in confusion.

Osborne must have his way. Even now, Alice kept the duke's balcony visit to herself. The impropriety would only distract from the truth: that the duke and Lady Windemere colluded to create Alice's ruin.

"I hope it is now clear why I cannot marry Lord Windemere. His mother arranged for the Duke of Cornwall to compromise me, just so Lord Windemere could 'save the day.' What we viewed as gallantry was really pre-arranged. If it weren't for Lady Windemere's plotting, I likely would be preparing to marry the Duke of Cornwall."

The fire crackled as Alice awaited a response. She felt nauseous, now that she had laid it all out plain as day.

Margot was the first to speak. "Do you want to marry the Duke of Cornwall?"

"I do not." The flipside of this plot, of course, was that the duke was willing to play Lady Windemere's puppet. He'd agreed to ruin Alice, for whatever reason. But Alice's heart had already recovered from the cruel twist of the duke's lips as he ignored her presence; the new implications barely bruised her.

"Do you care for Lord Windemere?" her sister followed up.

Oh, how Alice wished the answer were no. "It doesn't matter. I cannot marry him when his mother planned my ruin."

"Plenty of mothers plot for marriages," Lady Eastley protested. "That doesn't mean Lady Windemere meant for the duke to be so dishonorable. This is our neighbor, you remember. I cannot believe she would have the heart for the scheme you imagine."

"Can you not? Haven't you heard about the housekeeper she threw out on the street, after hiring a gentleman to put the housekeeper in a compromising position?"

Alice's mother admonished her with consternation now. "Considering the housekeeper went on to marry said gentleman, I don't give much credit to that rumor, and neither should you."

Alice hadn't heard that part of the story. But still: *Osborne must have his way.*

"Besides, as you said, Lady Windemere was trying to warn you away from the Duke of Cornwall, not push you into his arms." Her father stood. "Your logic is specious. The facts remain: you must marry, or you truly will be ruined. Osborne is a good man. Don't tie yourself into knots over some imaginary plan when you have a good fate right in front of you."

Alice squared her shoulders. "The fact remains: I will not marry him."

And so, they descended into a night of arguing. Debating. Crying. Arguing again. Her father yelled. Her mother soothed. Margot joked. All of it in vain as they chased each other in verbal circles. Alice would not marry Lord Windemere; she had no choice.

It was three in the morning – just an hour before springtime dawn – when Stuggins interrupted, looking very much as if he had stuffed his uniform on while rolling out of bed. "Beg your pardon, my lord, but you have just received a note from Lord Pemberly."

Lord Eastley took the note offered by the butler. "Thank you, Stuggins. Go back to rest now, please."

"There's no good news that couldn't wait for morning," Lady Eastley murmured. Alice watched her parents share a look. In just that one instant, with no words exchanged, they had a conversation.

She'd hoped to have that kind of relationship with

her husband. But if the evening had made anything clear to her, it was that she was to have no husband. Once the Marchioness of Leighster heard the marriage was off, word of her ruin would spread, and Alice would be retired to a nice cottage on the lake, with nothing but embroidery and books to keep her company.

It would be better than marrying a puppet.

Her father – who had spent so much of the evening red in the face from anger – went pale as he read the note. He handed it to his wife. Then he set his eyes on Alice.

"Lord Windemere has challenged the Duke of Cornwall to a duel. They fight at dawn."

The words echoed in Alice's ears as she tried to make sense of them. *Hugh* had challenged the Duke of Cornwall?

He wouldn't win. He had to know that. The Duke of Cornwall was a war hero. Hugh probably hadn't shot a gun in years.

Was this a message to her? Was he trying to demonstrate his love? Or a suicide mission?

Or perhaps it wasn't about her at all. Hugh had maintained that the Duke of Cornwall harbored a rivalry against him. Perhaps, throughout the whole Season, Alice had merely been a pawn. An object they could fight over.

To settle the rivalry once and for all.

"The challenge happened at White's when the Duke of Cornwall questioned Alice's virtue. Nearly everyone in the club heard," Lord Eastley was saying.

"Which means everyone in the *ton* will smell a scandal," Lady Eastley said. Sitting next to Alice, she cupped a hand over Alice's.

"Perhaps you won't have to marry Lord Windemere after all." Margot meant it as a joke.

But Alice couldn't stomach even the hint that Hugh might die. No matter that she couldn't marry him. No matter that the fight wasn't really, truly about her.

He wasn't going to die in a duel. And certainly not at the hands of the unworthy Duke of Cornwall.

Alice shot to her feet. "We have to stop him."

Chapter Twenty-Seven

Battersea Fields at dawn was nothing but a wet field of fog. As morning light slowly glowed through the mist, Hugh could see a tree here and there. A general black mass that was the city behind them. A lone carriage rumbling up the muddy path.

Hugh had arrived early. There was nothing else for him to do. He'd named his seconds – Lord Pemberly and the Earl of Farleigh, a friend from Cambridge who supplied the dueling pistol. He'd written letters to Alice and his mother, in the likely case that he did not walk off the field. He'd tracked down his solicitor in the gambling den of Rooks' to make sure his will was in order.

He'd even walked past the Winpole house, dark and solemn and neat as its Mayfair neighbors. A different man, perhaps, would have thrown a pebble to her window. Or climbed the drainpipe to reach her ledge, just for a peek of beautiful, sleeping Alice.

Hugh was content to know she was near. No matter that she hated him. For that one minute that he stood at their gates, Alice was close. He willed her to feel his love, to know that he wanted only her heart to be as happy as his for that wonderful, short week when she had been thrilled to marry him.

And then he had turned away. Hopped on a hackney.

And made his way to Battersea.

Pemberly was the second to arrive, while the sky was still pitch black. He slapped Hugh on the shoulder. "You all right, old man?"

Hugh didn't have the heart for words. He nodded.

Pemberly took the cue for silence well. They sat together on the boot of his carriage, watching the sky lighten.

Hugh turned over his life, trying to understand how he had ended up at this precise moment. If he'd imagined his life, it had been long: inventions to improve his estate's efficiency, Parliamentary sessions to improve his country's laws, evenings to enjoy his family. Now it would end foolishly. But at least Alice's honor would be defended.

At least this strange feud with the Duke of Cornwall would end.

The lone carriage approaching rolled to a stop a handful of yards away. Hugh hoped it was Farleigh, arriving with the dueling pistol. The sky was still rising from dark to gray. It might yet be another half hour before Hugh had to face his maker.

But it wasn't Farleigh. The cloaked passenger descended with a glowing orange lantern that illuminated the coach's ornamentation: the Cornwall crest.

Pemberly assayed forward to confer with the duke. Hugh stayed on his perch on the boot of Pemberly's carriage. He summoned Alice's essence. If only he could clasp her warmth and intelligence and fiery conviction as a shield across his heart. It would be enough to repel any bullet.

If only.

Pemberly returned. "His seconds are here. We await Farleigh."

Hugh's bowels cramped. He wished he could vomit up his fear. So here they were. One step away from his fate.

The duke stood in a clump with his seconds. In the lantern light, Hugh could see his pistol gleam silver as he prepared it for the shot.

Hugh knew why he was on this field. The Duke of Cornwall wasn't satisfied to ruin Alice, or to give her the cut direct. He was determined to drag her through the mud. All because Hugh loved her.

What Hugh didn't know was why the duke cared. Why a schoolboy prank would have so affected a man who had all the power in the world. Who had surely faced worse demons on the battlefields of the West Indies. Who must have bigger problems to solve than revenge.

Hugh was going to die. He might as well know why.

Standing, he crossed the boggy yards to the duke's camp. The seconds stood to attention as Hugh approached. As if he were going to attack.

"Second thoughts, Osborne?" the duke sneered.

"Hardly. This duel has been a decade in the making." Hugh surprised himself by meaning his bravado.

"Do you know what I'm going to do, when I've killed you?" Cornwall flipped his pistol in his hand as he spoke, as if it were a toy. "First, I'll have myself a nice cup of tea. Then, I'll go to the Winpole house. Climb straight up to Alice's balcony. Just imagine the welcome I'll get when I bring the good news that she doesn't have to marry you after all."

Hugh bristled at her name coming from Cornwall's filthy lips.

"I know that balcony well, of course. I was just there a few days ago. Commiserating with your fiancée about her destiny."

He was lying. He had to be. Hugh didn't know whether Alice's bedroom even had a balcony. It was simply one more taunt, one more punch to throw because Cornwall could.

Well, Hugh was sick and tired of being the one to hold his punches. "Just curious, Cornwall. Of all the enemies you must have, why did you honor me with your obsession? A decade is a long time to carry a grudge for a harmless prank."

The duke advanced, chest puffed out. A day ago, Hugh likely would have backed off. But he had nothing left to lose. No matter how much taller or stronger or angrier his opponent.

"Your impertinence astounds me. At school, I was eighth in line to the throne. Now, I am seventh. And yet you – generations away from any kind of power – dared try humiliate me in front of the school. The twelve-year-old earl thought he had some kind of power, didn't he? Thought he was smarter than his head boy. Thought you were better, just because you didn't have to wait as long for your incompetent father to die off, didn't you? Well, you still haven't learned your lesson." Cornwall huffed a sour, drunken breath at Hugh. "Anything you desire. Anything you care for. Are all mine. Because I am your superior."

Hugh nearly smiled. What perfect, hateful ammunition to help him walk onto that field and defy everyone's expectations. He would hit the duke with his bullet if it was the last thing he did.

"Your life must be exceptionally sad, if you've nothing better to do than sit around and covet mine. A mere earl."

The duke had begun to walk back to his clump. But at Hugh's taunt, he turned. His teeth flashed in the lantern light as he snarled. In an elegant, practiced motion, he wrested the pistol from his waist. Aimed it at Hugh.

And shot.

Chapter Twenty-Eight

Seeing as Pemberly didn't tell them where either Hugh or the duel were, the Winpole family did not have many recourses to find and stop it. Still, Alice did her best. She dispatched Lord Eastley to check any place a gentleman might go before a duel. The ladies would go to the Osborne house.

What Alice would say if she found him, she wasn't yet sure. But she had to try.

Lights on at the Osborne townhouse indicated someone was already up and about when the Winpole ladies heaved the iron knocker at the door. Alby answered with smooth clothes and brushed hair; they hadn't roused him from bed.

"Is Lord Windemere at home?" Alice asked. Even her own ears could hear the desperation in her voice. She didn't care. The sooner she could ascertain Hugh's safety, the better.

He wasn't going to die on her account.

"He is not, my lady," Alby said. "However, Lady Windemere would be delighted to receive you."

He led them upstairs, where Alice had not yet been, to a sitting room adjoining Lady Windemere's bedroom.

If one did not know the time, one might have assumed it was regular calling hours. Lady Windemere wore a fashionable morning dress, her hair was coiffed in a complicated chignon, and she served from a fresh tea service. She invited them to sit.

"You have heard about the duel," she stated without preamble.

"We are heartsick," Lady Eastley said. "Lady Windemere, I can only imagine how upset you are."

The countess did not acknowledge the sentiment. She set her dark, accusatory gaze on Alice. "My son would never have demanded satisfaction over any infraction before he decided to marry you. I hope you know what you're doing."

Alice wished she did, too. "Has he been here tonight? We mean to stop him from seeing through the duel."

"He has not. I doubt he will. He knows I would not allow him to leave again." Lady Windemere handed Alice a cup of tea. It was fixed to Hugh's liking: three lumps of sugar and milk.

Tears flooded her eyes. "I didn't want this to happen."

Lady Windemere looked skeptical. "Perhaps you should explain why you chose to run into the streets this afternoon. It rather upset Lord Windemere."

Alice looked to her mother and Margot. Lady Eastley raised an eyebrow. Margot lifted her shoulders infinitesimally.

In other words, it was up to her.

Alice stared into her teacup. "To be frank, Lady

Windemere, I overheard your conversation with Hugh – I mean, Lord Windemere - which confirmed my fears. I know that your ladyship plotted with the Duke of Cornwall to put me in a compromising position, so that Lord Windemere could offer for my hand and I'd be forced to accept."

There. She'd said it.

Now Alice found the courage to raise her eyes to Lady Windemere's. She braced for cutting hate, or ferocious anger, or even indifferent coolness.

She didn't expect despair.

"You're a foolish girl," Lady Windemere said, but her voice cracked in heartbreak as she said it. "And I'm a foolish mother."

Her body heaved with coughs. Lady Eastley rose, trying to place a hand on Lady Windemere's back, only to be waved off. Lady Windemere hacked into her handkerchief, then, presently, looked back to Alice.

"I wished Hugh to find a wife, yes. I asked him as we prepared for the Season if there wasn't anyone who caught his eye. He named you."

Alice's stomach turned. Even before their first dance at that first ball...Hugh had cared for her?

"In that sense, yes, I plotted. I found out which events your family planned to attend, and I pushed Hugh to go as well. He only listened to me half the time. Frankly, he didn't think he stood a chance against the Duke of Cornwall. I believe he was correct.

"I warned you off the Duke of Cornwall because I was truly concerned. Of course, I hoped you would notice Hugh instead, but that was only a small hope. I feared the duke would abuse you, for he's not only a rake. He takes anything Hugh loves and dashes it to pieces.

"The duke tormented Hugh at school. He was viciously jealous that Hugh already had his title and was smart to boot. They only shared one year there together, yet for years, the duke has sent me letters, fabricating deviant behavior on Hugh's part. He tried to prevent Hugh from getting a spot at Cambridge. Only because I called in a favor with my brother, the Duke of Hampshire, did Hugh make it in. Cornwall even told the Prince of Wales that Hugh plans to start a peasant revolt.

"Remember, Miss Winpole, the duke only asked you to dance after Hugh had already done so. He saw Hugh express an interest, and he swooped in to ruin you, just as he ruins everything else Hugh cares for."

Alice had never thought of that. Her skin pebbled with goosebumps. After all that she knew about the Duke of Cornwall – after experiencing his cut direct herself – did she really believe he would have needed to plot with Lady Windemere to decide Alice wasn't worth his time?

"I don't suppose you have any reason to believe me. If I were you, with the dark suspicions you harbor, I wouldn't believe me on my word alone. Unfortunately, my word is all I can offer.

"Still, let's say you're right. Let's say I plotted so that

you would marry Hugh. Is that so awful that you must run out on the street? I am dying. Even if you hate me with the fire of a thousand suns, you must only put up with me for a matter of months. Then you will be all Hugh has left. Is it really so awful that you must throw a fit?"

As if conjuring her sickness, Lady Windemere descended into coughing again. Alice flinched. Her family had said much the same a hundred times already. But to hear it from the dying woman herself...

Everything Lady Windemere said so far rang true. The whole affair had never made sense to Alice because she didn't understand the duke's motives. But in the lens of a sick rivalry, the episodes that had so tormented her settled together like puzzle pieces. That the Duke of Cornwall would compromise her – even try to tempt her into an extramarital affair – in order to torment Hugh made more sense than that he would do so on some directive from Lady Windmere.

Which meant that Alice had caused all this upheaval for nothing.

Done coughing, Lady Windemere tucked her handkerchief into her pocket. "I have never seen my son happier than the morning he announced to me that he was engaged to marry you. That was not me plotting. It was Hugh, falling in love with you. I could only pray you would in turn see all there is to love about him."

These last words settled as an accusation. Alice deserved them. He *did* love her. He showered her with love.

And now he was off to a duel, and she'd never so much as hinted that she loved him back.

She looked up to Lady Windemere. "What do we do now?"

Hugh's mother poured another cup of tea. She dumped in three sugary lumps. And she looked out the window. "We wait."

Chapter Twenty-Nine

Hugh had been in the middle of a dream. The details were fuzzy, as consciousness returned, but he remembered chasing Alice up the green hill at Richmond Hall. Her bright white dress flapped always just out of reach. She'd looked over her shoulder, laughing. Was it at him, or with him? He couldn't tell. He'd only wanted to catch up to her.

And now the dream was over. He was in his solid body, which seared with pain. His eyelids were heavy, too thick to open. Wherever he was smelled of a warm coal fire and lavender water and tangy, metallic blood.

His blood, he supposed. Now that he was awake, he remembered that he'd been shot. At close range. In the arm. It would have been in the heart or stomach or gut, but somehow, Hugh had jumped to the side as the Duke of Cornwall drew the pistol.

Apparently, he had survival reflexes after all.

Now he could hear murmurs around him, in addition to the crackling of the fire and the steady, muted sounds of the city outside. He focused on the voices: female, hushed, and worried. Not his mother, who couldn't whisper if she tried. Perhaps a nursemaid. Hugh suddenly remembered his governess from years ago, let go after his sister Mary died, who had been so frightened and yet so determined to sit by the children's sickbeds as they struggled through fever.

The smell of lavender water grew stronger, and suddenly a wet cloth pressed against his forehead. Hugh jerked in surprise. His eyes found the strength to open.

And look directly into eyes as green as a country lane.

Alice drew her hand back instantly. She blinked, startled, and then she smiled. "You're awake."

Hugh would do anything if only she'd keep smiling at him like that. He sought for something witty to say, but only ended with, "You're in my bedroom."

"Unfortunately, she is chaperoned," came a second voice. Hugh turned his head – oh, how sore was his neck – to see Margot seated on the other side of his bed. She winked at him. "Still two days until the wedding, after all."

Two days. The duel had rounded out Sunday, and the wedding was scheduled for Saturday, which meant Hugh had lost three days. To sleep? To fever? He looked back to Alice, his anchor.

"You've been fighting a fever for quite some time now. Lady Windemere says it's a good sign because it means your body is healing, and that you've always been a bully to fevers." Alice set down her bowl of lavender water. "I'll ring for her. She will be so glad to hear you've woken."

Lady Windemere was indeed glad to see Hugh awake. So glad that it was only after she shooed away the

Winpole sisters, examined his wound, patted ointment on his chapped lips, and called in a tray of oxtail broth for strength that she scolded him.

"Whatever were you thinking? Challenging a bully to a duel. I never thought a son of mine would be so foolish."

Considering Hugh hadn't expected to live long enough to be scolded again by his mother, he was quite glad to receive it. "It was inconsiderate to you, I admit. Unfortunately, the duke simply said things that cannot be forgiven. I was left no choice."

"There is always a choice." Lady Windemere set her fierce dark stare on him. "But I trust you made the right one. In any case, it has all worked out for us. All of London knows what a dishonorable man the duke is, to fire at you before the duel even started. As long as you live through it, you will remain my favorite son."

Hugh eased into a sitting position, roaring with pain as he did so. His arm did not like any movement whatsoever.

"Thank you for letting Alice look after me."

His mother set her lips in a firm, straight line. Actually, if Hugh wasn't entirely wrong, they quirked a little upwards. As if into a smile. "She and I have made our peace. I still think she is a headstrong, fanciful girl, and I suspect she still thinks I'm a severe old shrew. But we found we can agree when it comes to you."

Hugh could imagine the two getting on just fine, in a few months perhaps, once they had a chance to get to know each other.

If they had a few months together.

He took another spoonful of broth to satisfy his mother. Then he rested his head on the silk pillowcase. "Is she still here?"

"She has refused to go home," Lady Windemere said. "I told her she didn't have a right to a room just yet, but all the same, she has remained. Ladies Sybil and Margot take turns visiting, to make sure she isn't a complete nuisance."

"Perhaps I could speak to her?"

"Perhaps you could." Rising, Lady Windemere tottered toward the bell pull. "Perhaps I could entice Lady Wickham to help me inspect my jewelry in the meantime. I have wanted to review it before the wedding, and I need a set of young eyes to help me."

Alby arrived, to escort Lady Windemere in a wheeled chair through the house. She gave Hugh one last severe glare. "Be sure she closes the door when she comes in, to keep the healthy air in this room. I won't have you dying because your fiancée was silly enough to let out the healing airs."

Hugh smiled. In his condition, he could hardly do much damage to Alice's virtue, but he appreciated his mother's willingness to allow it.

After all, it wasn't every day one saw the lady who one just took a bullet for.

Now that he was fully awake, Hugh realized he

hardly looked the part of handsome and put-together gentleman. Grimacing against the pain in his arm, he took advantage of the few minutes alone to run his fingers through his hair, wipe the crust from his eyes, and assemble his nightshirt so it wasn't quite so crumpled.

It was the best he could do.

Alice knocked on the door before entering. The firelight cast her in a soft, orange glow. Her skin was luminous; her hair nearly glittered. She wore a loose, pale morning gown. He hadn't seen her in such casual clothes before, yet this was the view he'd likely grow used to, once they were married.

If they got married.

She settled on the chair at his side. "How are you feeling?"

"Better every minute." Hugh soaked up her presence. She wore a peaceful expression, but Hugh had the sensation it had been smoothed on to hide an undercurrent of nerves. He wanted to take her hand. Instead, he said stupidly, "How are you feeling?"

Alice looked down at her hands. "I suppose I feel guilty. I'm told the whole duel was to defend my honor, even after I've been so awful to you."

"You could cast me in the gutter, and I'd still defend your honor."

"Even though you know very well that I actually have very little virtue left?" Alice's gaze winged up at him from beneath her lashes. Hugh revised his wishes.

He didn't want to hold her hand.

He wanted to kiss her endlessly.

"It's the principle of the thing," he managed to say.

Alice looked away. "I'm sorry for how I ran out of here that day. Even in that state of mind, I should have been more ladylike."

"I don't care about ladylike. I was worried for your safety." Not to mention concerned for his own heart. *I won't marry into a family that plots...* "Are you still upset?"

She shook her head. "When I heard about the duel, I realized how silly I was being. You have been nothing but wonderful to me. Why should I get so upset over something that *may* have happened, when I know how lucky I am for what actually happened?"

Hugh waited for more. He wasn't sure what he expected her to say, but he sensed she had something else, some deeper thought lingering on the tip of her tongue.

But Alice only stared at her hands in her lap. Hugh reached his good palm towards her. "I'm told you haven't gone home since the duel."

"Lady Windemere says I'm impertinent." Alice reported it with a smile. She took his hand. Neither of them wore a glove; he thought his skin might burn from the fire she ignited with her touch.

"Let's not bring my mother into this." His voice came out in a hoarse croak.

Leaning forward, Alice murmured, "I do believe a

gentleman is owed a kiss after defending a lady's virtue."

Her lips were warm as they landed a soft, thoughtful kiss on his. His hand locked around her neck by instinct, so that even when she parted, she was only a breath away. Hugh sought out her luminous green eyes again, so bright and sure. And, in that moment, a little bit sultry.

He pulled her down for more. He was suddenly ravenous, for her kiss, for her touch, for her everything. He traced his hand down to hers, lacing his fingers with hers. She smelled so sweet and yet her body was firm as it sank against his. Alice purred as their kiss grew deeper, more ferocious. Her free hand threaded through his hair. Instantly, every nerve stood on end, awaiting her caress.

"Would it be terribly forward of me if I repositioned for a better angle?" Alice whispered, her breath licking his ear.

"I'll challenge anyone who thinks to question you on it," Hugh said. He claimed another kiss as she climbed from the chair onto the bed. Now she straddled him, nothing between them but her light muslin skirt and the thin bedsheets.

Alice's mouth roamed from Hugh's lips downwards. She pressed kisses along his jaw, his neck, stamped the hollow of his clavicle where his nightshirt revealed his curling chest hair. Hugh reached his good arm around to cup her backside, which was deliciously soft in his palm. Alice hummed in pleasure.

"Are you in any pain?" she asked as she returned her

attention to his lips, dotting kisses between her words.

"None." It was true: the gunshot had vanished from his consciousness with her touch. "You're the only laudanum I need."

Alice breathed in a kiss as response, deepening it in ferocity until she bit his lip. Hugh's whole body responded. She would feel his excitement against her thigh, but he couldn't muster up any regret. He ran his hand up her waist, exploring her figure curving underneath the dress, and settled on her breast, which he remembered so well from their carriage ride. He pressed a kiss to her nipple through the muslin fabric.

Straightening – still tantalizingly sitting atop his manhood – Alice reached behind and started unbuttoning her dress. Hugh couldn't think to stop her. He only watched as her breasts strained against the fabric, then dropped loose as she pulled the dress overhead and tossed it to the end of the bed.

She took off her stays next, and then her chemise. Before he could believe it, she straddled him without a stitch of clothing.

And so incredibly beautiful.

Hugh sat up, ignoring the flare of pain from his arm, so he could appreciate her from up close. He kissed her pert, soft breasts in their freedom. He explored the heat of her skin. He cupped her full, naked bottom and listened to the gasp of pleasure that escaped her throat. He couldn't help himself from whispering, "I love you, Alice."

She didn't whisper back. She only pushed him into the pillows and drew back the bedcovers. His nightshirt had already worked itself up around his waist; from there below he was as naked as she. Alice grasped his length in her warm, soft hand. Hugh nearly blacked out from pleasure.

Then she lowered herself slowly onto him. She was so wet and tight. Hugh had never felt such a perfect pleasure. Until she started to rock. It was instinctual, a little out of rhythm, but Hugh felt nothing except the sensation. He locked his good arm around her waist to keep her there as they found a mutual rhythm. He kissed her greedily. This was Alice. His love.

Their speed increased as Hugh felt himself nearing his end. Releasing her waist, he slid his good thumb onto her wet nub and started slow circles. Alice jerked in surprise, then melted, losing all control over her hips as Hugh lathered her into a frenzy. He started circling his hips to match his thumb until finally, suddenly, she shuddered her way into a *petit mort*.

Hugh followed her just a moment later, as she fell into his chest. The world disappeared for a moment into nothing but pleasure.

And then it returned, in the form of Alice's perfect, beautiful smile.

She lay nestled against him on the sliver of mattress to his left, his good side. Hugh dotted a kiss to her nose. "I love you," he said again, too happy to worry about his words.

She pecked his cheek in return. "I suppose we'll have to get married now."

He blinked. She'd said the words in good cheer, perhaps as a joke. But the verbiage gave him pause. Had she still been considering not marrying him?

And was she only marrying him because she felt she had to?

Unbidden, Hugh remembered the duke's taunts on Battersea Field. *I was on that balcony just a few days ago, commiserating about her fate.*

"Does your bedroom have a balcony?"

Alice blinked. For just an instant, her whole expression tightened with guilt. Then she smoothed it with a smile. "Yes. Why?"

It could have been a coincidence. A lucky guess on Cornwall's part.

But Hugh was a student of mathematics and philosophy. It was more likely that Cornwall spoke in specifics because they were true.

Which meant as recently as the previous week, Alice had been entertaining Cornwall in the privacy of her balcony.

Because she didn't want to marry Hugh. She wanted to marry Cornwall.

Hugh had offered marriage, declared his love, and faced his own death, all for her. Alice dithered between sweet, hot kisses and dashing out to the street in furies. And Hugh was no longer sure he wanted to settle for a wife who viewed him as her escape from ruin.

"We don't have to marry, if you don't want to."

Alice, curled against his chest, stilled, like prey who realizes it is being hunted. She didn't look him in the eyes. "What do you mean?"

"Marrying you would make me the happiest man alive, as long as it's what you really, truly want. But if I am just..." Hugh couldn't say it with her so close. He pushed into a seated position. Pain seared from his shoulder across his chest. "If you are only marrying me out of convenience, I'd rather you let me be."

Alice spilled off the bed as he moved, landing naked on her feet. She started throwing on her clothes in a frenzy. "How can you say that?"

"I won't tell a soul about it," Hugh said, turning his head away to give her privacy. "I'm not interested in causing scandal for you. It's only that..." He trailed off because he couldn't quite find the words to say what he really meant. That his heart wasn't strong enough to watch his wife wither in unhappiness, if marriage really wasn't what she wanted.

"You can marry Cornwall, or you won't have to marry at all," he said. "I arranged in my will to leave you with an income, expecting I'd die in the duel, so you can live independently. I'll gladly settle it on you now, if it's what you prefer."

"You can't think I still feel for Cornwall, after he gave me the cut direct. After he tried to kill you!" All buttoned up now, Alice moved into his line of sight. Fury lit her eyes brighter than any fire.

How Hugh wished she felt that same passion for him.

"The choice is yours, Alice. If you marry me, do it because you care for me. I'd prefer to see you happy – even if it means you marry a man you do love – than trapped by my side."

Alice set her hands on her hips as she glared at him. "We are getting married in two days, Lord Windemere."

"Then think on it for two days. If you don't come to the wedding, I'll understand."

She opened her mouth, as if to say something else, then stopped. Summoning herself ever straighter, Alice dipped a curtsy. "You are overtired. Get some rest. I'll see you on Saturday."

Hugh stared at the door even after she sealed him in. Alice in all her fierceness was the loveliest woman on earth. He likely wouldn't see her again, except perhaps crossing paths at large social functions.

But he was at peace with that. He would remember her like she'd been today – caring, sultry, furious – and hope she was happy, whatever she chose.

One day, Hugh might even be happy again. But that didn't matter quite so much.

Chapter Thirty

Alice didn't know why she hadn't said it. It was only three little words. *I love you.* It had been on the tip of her tongue as she apologized for her behavior. But as the words surged forward, some strange fear had muted her, so that instead, she threw herself at him like a harlot.

Oh, and every time Hugh had whispered it to her – *I love you, Alice* – she'd grown just a little bit lighter and brighter. She wanted to say it back. She wanted him to know how she felt.

After all, from the moment he'd been carried into the house by Lords Pemberly and Farleigh, blood dripping across the parquet, Alice had *known*. Deep in her bones, with certainty. She loved him.

And yet, she couldn't say it.

Especially not when she needed to. When Hugh hooded his eyes from her and said such strange, noble things. He didn't want to marry her if she didn't love him back.

He didn't think she loved him.

In the carriage ride back to the Winpole house, Alice told Margot about the conversation – eliminating the beautiful, wonderful, scandalous interlude when she'd devoured Hugh.

"Write him a letter telling him how you feel," Margot

advised. "You can hardly blame him for being confused, since you keep accusing him of this scheme or that."

"It was only ever one scheme." But Margot was right. How was Hugh to know how she felt when Alice herself had only just realized it?

She tried writing a letter. In between her final fittings, social calls, and overseeing the packing of her trousseau, Alice wrote draft after draft. Each one worse than the last.

My dearest Hugh.

My beloved.

You are the force that makes my heart beat.

It was all terrible dribble that sounded like she'd copied some unctuous poem. *She* didn't even believe herself when she saw it written out, so why would Hugh?

The trouble was, Alice didn't know how to articulate it to herself, much less anyone else. All she knew was Hugh filled her every thought. His name tattooed her every breath. She'd refused to leave the Osborne house not only because she feared for his life but because every last inch of her ached for him when she couldn't see him.

Alice shifted to the concept of demonstrating her love with gifts. Flowers were too feminine. Books were too hard to arrange when she didn't know what he already owned. Chocolate didn't seem intimate enough.

Her best idea was to build him a machine. She even found a book in her father's library on pulleys and levers to see if she could fit one together. But even if she did, how would she tell him it was a representation of her love?

Too soon, it was the morning of her wedding, and she still hadn't told Hugh she loved him.

They'd arranged a small ceremony at the cathedral. Margot and Lisbeth attended Alice, while Lords Pemberly and Farleigh stood up with Hugh. Lady Windemere sat with her brother, the Duke of Hampshire, in the family pew, while Alice's parents were accompanied by Margot's husband, the Earl of Wickham, and Lord Eastley's three sisters.

Alice heart hammered as she walked down the aisle at Lord Eastley's arm. Hugh stood straight as a stick at the altar; even from the back of the church, Alice could read his nerves. She only hoped her presence answered his question.

She wanted to marry him.

She chose to marry him.

Yet when Lord Eastley placed her hand in Hugh's, she saw only confusion in Hugh's eyes. Or perhaps it was disbelief.

She squeezed his palm as he guided her to the altar. He didn't squeeze it back, instead letting his good hand drop to his side. Alice gripped her bouquet of lilies and fuchsia.

She would have their whole life to prove to him she loved him.

But throughout mass, Hugh avoided her gaze. His face was shuttered in the unfriendly mask Alice associated with Lady Windemere. Alice wanted to whisk him away to a private room. She'd slap him, or kiss him, or both. Anything to shock him into listening to her. Into seeing her.

Was this how he'd felt, when she had pushed him away?

They were close to the end of the ceremony now. Soon, Alice would pledge her life to Hugh's, and he would vow to protect her. She had chosen to be here. Didn't he see what that meant?

Weren't her actions enough?

The rector cleared his throat. "If any of you know cause or just impediment why these two persons should not be joined together in Holy Matrimony, so declare it."

The cathedral resounded in silence. No one even sniffled.

The rector opened his mouth to continue the ceremony.

"I object."

Everyone stared at her. Alice would stare at herself, too, if she could. Surely, she was the first bride in history to object to her own matrimony.

Hugh, for his part, winced. If before he'd been a blank mask, now he was the picture of resignation. He thought she was objecting because she didn't actually want to marry him.

Alice took a deep breath. It was now or never.

"I object because Lord Windemere thinks I am marrying him out of convenience. It is my fault entirely because I have been absolutely terrible and ungrateful toward him. My lord, you are right. I cannot marry you under these circumstances."

Hugh watched her with wide, wary eyes. Winking at him, Alice handed her bouquet to Margot, knelt, and took Hugh's good hand in hers. They both wore gloves, but she could feel the heat of his palm. The strength of his magic fingers.

Oh, she hoped he'd believe her now.

"Lord Windemere, you once described for me your ideal countess. I never answered your question about my ideal husband. Here is my answer: he is kind and intelligent. He wants to improve the lot of the common man with new inventions. He honors his mother. He is wickedly clever if you catch him alone. And he values my happiness above his own, even if he's being terribly stupid about it.

"My lord, I love you desperately. I haven't shown it well so far, but if you let me, I'll devote every day of the rest of our lives to proving myself. Would you do me the honor of marrying me?"

Hugh was trying very hard to keep a *ton*-appropriate emotionless mask, but his beam shone through. Then he gave up the charade altogether and let out a laugh. "Yes." He tugged her to her feet. "Thank you for asking."

Their guests, not quite knowing what to do, applauded. Alice barely heard, she was so caught up in Hugh.

If only they weren't in church, she'd devour him all over again.

He whispered, "You're terribly forward, my lady."

Alice grinned. She would be terribly forward with him every day from now on, whether he liked it or not.

Epilogue

The wedding breakfast could have ended as soon as it started, in Hugh's opinion, but instead it stretched a full three hours. There were the champagne toasts, the cutting of the cake, Lord Eastley falling out of his chair on account of too much merriness. Miss Lisbeth Dawes – newly engaged herself to Lord Gresham – pulled Alice aside to giggle in a corner, and then so did Lady Wickham. Pemberly and Farleigh ribbed Hugh about Alice's speech.

But finally, the guests trickled away. Lady Windemere was the last to go, as she was staying the week with the Duke of Hampshire. She slipped her hand into Hugh's for farewell. "That scene in the church was absolutely scandalous. However, I am glad to know you two will be happy together."

"Just as you plotted," Alice said with a giggle. Lady Windemere raised her chin haughtily, but a smile twinkled in her eye.

"There is one piece of advice I have for you to keep your husband happy: always serve his tea the way he likes. Three quarters tea, one quarter milk –"

"And three lumps of sugar," Alice finished.

Hugh hated to disappoint two ladies, but more, he hated the prospect of that concoction for the rest of his life. "Actually, Mother, my preference as an adult is black tea. Perhaps a dash of milk, if I haven't eaten a meal recently."

His mother stared at him. For a moment, he thought she was going to correct him. But she merely kissed him on the cheek. "I'll see you in a week."

With that, Alby whisked her away to an awaiting carriage.

The house was finally empty of guests.

Hugh turned to Alice. His wife. She was radiant. Her eyes sparkled as she smiled up at him, and he remembered how jealous he had been after that first ball, when she had bestowed her gaze to the Duke of Cornwall instead.

He'd been right to be jealous. She was worth it.

And now she loved him. Hugh Osborne, Earl of Windemere, had somehow earned the love of this beautiful, forceful creature.

He could scarcely believe it.

"What shall we do now, Countess? Tour the house? Walk about the gardens? Play some parlor games?"

Alice placed a finger to her mouth, feigning thought. "Whatever we do, I'd like to change my clothes. I'll need your help though."

Hugh loved his wicked, forward wife. "It's the gentlemanly thing to do."

Pasting on a chaste expression, Alice started up the stairs. "And then perhaps I can start my mission to prove my love to you. I have some ideas for where to start."

"Oh, do you?" Hugh followed her, ready to leap the stairs two at a time. But he didn't need to run to catch her. Alice waited patiently, eager to be at his side.

He kissed her, no matter if the servants saw.

They ran the rest of the way up hand-in-hand.